"I must accept the parson's word about what transpired between you." Papa spoke directly to Beatrice.

"But I will not suffer that young farmer to speak against me. What did he say?"

"Surely that is a private matter between the two young people," Mrs. Cabot said.

"He said"—Beatrice raised her voice over Mrs. Cabot's objection—"that no matter what his feelings toward me may be, he refused to ask me to act against your wishes." Her voice came close to breaking into tears.

"That is well." Papa stared at the tea cup in his hand as if ready to throw it against the fireplace. "These are my wishes. I forbid you to speak to him or see him again. The man is not fit to be the husband of my daughter." He returned the cup to Mrs. Cabot. "I'm afraid I have no taste for tea this afternoon. Come, Beatrice, we are finished here."

Award-winning author and speaker **DARLENE FRANKLIN** recently returned to cowboy country— Oklahoma. The move was prompted by her desire to be close to her son's family; her daughter Jolene has preceded her into glory.

Darlene loves music, needlework, reading, and reality TV. Talia, a Lynx point Siamese cat, proudly claims Darlene as her person.

Darlene has published several titles with Barbour Publishing, most recently, *A Woodland Christmas*. *Bridge to Love* is the sequel to *Prodigal Patriot*, two of three romances set in the Green Mountain State. Visit Darlene's blog at www.darlenefranklinwrites.blogspot. com for information on book giveaways and upcoming titles.

Books by Darlene Franklin

HEARTSONG PRESENTS
HP650—Romanian Rhapsody
HP855—Beacon of Love
HP911—The Prodigal Patriot

Bridge to
Love

Darlene Franklin

Heartsong Presents

To my mother, who taught me how to keep on going even when it seems impossible, and now cheers me on from the sidelines in heaven.

A note from the Author:
I love to hear from my readers! You may correspond with me by writing:

Darlene Franklin
Author Relations
PO Box 721
Uhrichsville, OH 44683

ISBN 978-1-61626-078-1

BRIDGE TO LOVE

All scripture quotations are taken from the King James Version of the Bible.

All of the characters and events in this book are fictitious. Any resemblance to actual persons, living or dead, or to actual events is purely coincidental.

Our mission is to publish and distribute inspirational products offering exceptional value and biblical encouragement to the masses.

PRINTED IN THE U.S.A.

Author's note

In April 1815 a volcano erupted east of Java, far removed from western civilization. Slowly winds carried volcanic dust around the world, disrupting weather patterns as they went. In 1816 temperatures dropped significantly across the northeastern United States and Northern Europe. Frost and/or summer snow killed crops every month during the short growing season. Famine and starvation dogged the rugged New Englanders, so much so that many people emigrated to warmer climes. The year 1816 became known as "The Poverty Year," "The Year of No Summer," and even as "Eighteen Hundred and Froze to Death."

Calvin Tuttle used the same method to grow a successful crop as did real Vermonter Nathaniel Foster. Both of them also rejected offers for their seed corn of five dollars a bushel from the bank and instead sold it for one dollar to their neighbors. Foster's town became known as "Egypt," after the biblical story of Joseph and the famine.

one

"They're all dead!"

Beatrice Bailey shivered in her cotton dress outside her house on one side of the town square in Maple Notch, Vermont. She wanted to stomp her foot in frustration, but that was childish, as well as downright dangerous with the slippery snow under foot. "Oh, there you are." She found a sprig of purple lilacs to bring inside the house.

"What are you doing outside in this weather?"

Mama.

She continued fussing at Beatrice. "You don't even have a coat on. You'll catch your death of cold."

At Mama's reminder, Beatrice felt icy water seeping through the thin soles of her shoes. "I didn't expect it to be so chilly. The sun was shining yesterday."

Her mother shook her finger. "You're acting like you've never seen snow in May. It *does* happen."

Beatrice followed her mother into the kitchen, where Papa waited at the table.

Mama continued her tirade. "Mr. Bailey, what are we going to do with this girl? She went outside dressed like. . .this!"

Papa lifted his eyes from the newspaper—no doubt reading about the price of potash and other trade goods—and looked at

6

his daughter over his spectacles. He took them off and looked again, frowning. "Where *is* your coat, Beatrice? I won't have my daughter wandering around outside like a pauper's child."

"Oh, Papa." She gestured toward him with the flowers. "I only wanted to get some lilacs for the table. I know you like them, too." She frowned. "But the sprigs are all falling off our lovely bushes. All the white lilacs are gone, and most of the purple ones, too."

"Oh? Is that all? Well, they'll grow again next year."

"It's not only the lilacs. Last night's snow will have killed the baneberries and harebells as well. Not to mention the kitchen garden."

"Hmm." Papa had returned his attention to the paper.

"Papa!"

With a sigh, he set the paper down again. "Yes?"

"Can you pick up some more seeds for me the next time you go to Burlington?"

"Of course." He smiled at her, and she kissed him on the cheek. "Now may I read the paper in peace?" He buried his nose back in the page.

Beatrice stared out the window at the snow weighting down tree branches budding with the new year's growth. Last night's frost and snow would affect more than her flowers. Why, people said the maple sap hadn't been running true to form, and the freeze might stop the apple trees and cranberry bushes from bearing fruit.

Don't be a ninny. Snow did fall in Maple Notch in May from time to time.

The animals wouldn't like the cold weather either. Beatrice looked underneath the Franklin stove, one of the few in northern Vermont, her mother's pride and joy. Patches, their calico cat, had taken to sleeping there during cold snaps. After all, it was the warmest spot in the house, as Mama bragged. No black and brown tail slapped the floor, betraying her presence.

"Here, kitty, kitty. I've got some bacon for you." Beatrice dangled her hand near the floor, but the cat didn't appear. "Has anybody seen Patches?"

Papa snorted from behind the paper. "Not this morning. I'm sure she's fine."

"I do hope she's someplace warm." Patches ran out the door whenever it opened and might be caught in the snow.

"As soon as I'm finished, I'm going outside to look for her." Beatrice rushed through her plate of johnnycakes, eggs, and bacon. Mama would scold her if she left something uneaten. Five minutes after finishing her meal, Beatrice buttoned on her coat, taking the time to pull on her gloves and boots. Anything less, and both parents might make her stay inside. As soon as she opened the door, Patches darted inside and headed straight for the stove.

Papa drained his coffee cup. "Care to walk with me across the green?"

"Of course, Papa. I always do." No amount of snow could keep a born and bred Yankee inside very long.

"Your bonnet?" Mama asked, handing her a wide-brimmed hat that would protect her hair from falling snow. A part of Beatrice wished she could run across the common and catch the snow with her tongue as she had when she was a young girl. But no young woman of nineteen would behave in such a hoydenish way.

Still, Beatrice enjoyed the morning strolls. She suspected Papa liked her to accompany him to impress the people of

Maple Notch with her fine wardrobe—the best New York had to offer, often the latest fashions all the way from Paris. But Beatrice treasured their few quiet minutes together. Not often did she claim his entire attention.

"Have you given any further thought to my proposal?" Papa asked.

Beatrice dipped her head, glad for the bonnet that hid her expression. Papa wanted her to stay with her grandmother in New York for a time—this summer and fall, perhaps. He wished her to marry some well-to-do young man who could succeed him at the bank.

Beatrice had traveled to New York several times, but the city stifled her. Her home and gardens gave her ample pleasure, but she'd never been able to make her father understand. She sighed. "I'm happy right here. I don't want to go to a city among so many people. I'll lose myself."

Papa chuckled. "You don't have to worry. You'll be a lovely rose wherever you're planted, and you deserve to experience more of life than this." His arm swept around the view of the common.

The sight he dismissed so easily brought great joy to her own heart. She thought of her grandfather when she passed the statue commemorating the Green Mountain Boys who had fought with Ethan Allen. The meetinghouse where she had come to know the Lord had seen fifty years of weddings and funerals. The maple trees provided sweet sap in the spring and brilliant colors in the fall.

"Everything I want is here," she repeated.

"Only this morning I heard you complaining about the cold and snow." Father sneaked a sidewise glance at her. He was teasing her.

She giggled. "I confess I will be happy when summer comes."

❧

In spite of his boots and winter coat, Calvin Tuttle shivered—perhaps because he didn't have his mittens on. He couldn't examine the tender young plants with his hands covered. "Any luck yet?" He paused at the end of the row to ask his friend and partner, Tobias Heath.

"Nope. I'm hoping to find something here under the shelter of the trees where the snow didn't get so high. Maybe some of the seedlings survived." Tobias blew on his fingers.

"Maybe." Calvin joined him at the rim of the clearing and dug through the finger-numbing snow, still deep in spite of the protection of the trees. The tender shoots were frozen clear through, with that almost translucent color of ice. When he touched one, the bud where the ear of corn would eventually grow broke off in his hands.

Tobias brushed the snow aside to the bare ground, where they had planted potatoes for the eyes to sprout. One came up in his hand, blackened, shriveled roots dangling from the spud. The squash vines hadn't fared any better. "Maybe you can feed some of this to your animals." His voice sounded uncertain. "They must be getting as tired of this winter as we are."

"That reminds me. Keep an eye out for bear sign. If the storms are killing the wild plants, too, they're going to be searching for anything to eat, anything at all."

The two men continued working in silence. Calvin walked among the last of the plants with little hope, and found nothing to change his mind.

"Do you get these late storms a lot?" Tobias asked.

Calvin shrugged. "You ought to know. You're from Vermont, too."

"In town, though. I never was a farmer." Tobias slapped his hands together and thought about it. "Snow is as common on Easter as not. But I don't remember too many storms in May."

"It happens. We'll plant another crop and trust the good Lord to provide come harvest time."

"Not what you were hoping for, is it?" Tobias looked at him sideways as they walked in the direction of the cabin. "You told me that with the two of us working the land, we could make up for lost time. And now this." He gestured at the snow-covered fields.

Behind him in the forest, Calvin heard a tree branch cracking under the weight of the heavy spring snow, and he shook his head. "No use arguing with the Almighty."

"Yeah. We both know who would win that argument." Tobias grinned.

Beneath the teasing banter, Calvin heard the painful questions that plagued his friend. When they'd volunteered to serve in the army in the recent war with Britain, they'd known they'd see people die in battle. But they hadn't expected to see more people die of disease than from musket balls. Tobias had lost his sweetheart and come to Maple Notch to mend his broken heart.

No use thinking about that now. Calvin looked across the clearing where he sought to establish a farm of his own. This year's crop required extra care. He'd have to put off clearing more land and rooting out the tree stumps for another season.

"There's always next year," Tobias said.

"What, are you reading my mind now?"

"You always stop at that same spot and look over the fields.

It's not hard to guess what you're thinking."

Calvin began moving again. "The problem is I cleared this land back before the war. Then I joined the army, and the forest grew back over some of what I cleared. I've only had one full growing season."

"And you've got that bank payment on your mind. I know. But God will provide."

God had to. Or else Calvin might lose it all. He held no illusions.

The banker, Hiram Bailey, would demand every penny of the payment. He'd say he owed it to his investors. Little things like bad weather and poor crops didn't enter his calculations. Bailey had called a meeting of the farmers later in the day, and Calvin wondered what he would have to say.

The destruction wrought by the night's frost couldn't be undone. Calvin would have to replant, that was all, and work all the harder. Maybe he could speak with Pa about borrowing old Abe, the ox, so he could work faster. Turn the ruined plants under for mulch at least, to get some good out of it. Once he'd done that, hopefully the ground would be warm enough to replant.

Should he consider changing up his crops? Study on what yielded the highest profit? No, it wasn't prudent to try unproven crops in a year when everything seemed to be going wrong. Stick with what he knew worked in his fields. Corn, beans, and squash, as well as potatoes.

He stared to his right, at the smoke curling from his brother's chimney. To his left lay Uncle Stephen's cabin. No use wishing for an ox. They shared an ox between them. Most of the time it worked out fine, but the men with families to feed would need Abe first.

"Let's go get the plow and start to work." Calvin headed for the barn, with Tobias following. Midway to the door, he heard someone calling to him.

"Calvin! Mr. Heath! Wait up!"

Calvin turned around with a smile. Peggy Reid, his cousin, waved to him from the fence line.

"Ma said for you to come over today during the nooning. She told your brother Solomon earlier but wanted to be sure you knew about it."

Nice of Aunt Hilda to send them a personal invitation. Folks had been going back and forth between the Reid and Tuttle farms since the first settlers came to Maple Notch.

"Great. We'll be right there as soon as we clean up."

Peggy hesitated as if expecting him to say something more. When he didn't, she waved good-bye and headed in the direction of the Reids' cabin. He waited until she had gone a few yards before he called his greeting after her.

"Happy birthday!"

She grinned and waved.

Peggy was all of nineteen today. He wouldn't have many more celebrations with his cousin before some man came along and claimed her. He glanced at Tobias and wondered. His friend deserved some happiness after losing his sweetheart.

"Let's get going," he told Tobias. "We can grab her gift later."

After the celebration, he would bring up the problems with the crops with the family. Maybe together they could come up with a solution.

≈

The morning had turned out ever so nice, so much better than Beatrice had feared when she walked to the bank with her father early in the day. Today was her best friend's birthday, and she had never missed a single celebration with Peggy Reid, not once since they started school together all those years ago. A few inches of snow on the ground wouldn't keep her at home.

"Mama, I need to head over to the Reid farm today."

"In this weather? Don't be foolish."

Predictable. "It's Peggy's birthday today. And look, the sun has come out and it's turned out to be a lovely day. I'll ride Princess, so I won't get all dirty."

"Very well. Just be sure that you're home well before dark and presentable before supper." Mama smiled. "You know how your father gets when you go out visiting the farms."

"Why, the road goes straight through the woods. It's not dark and dangerous like it was when he was a boy. Besides, I've been there hundreds of times." Papa would prefer she not have any friends with "that sort." The problem was, then she'd have no friends at all.

"He only wants the best for you, young missy." Mama's smile was gentle, taking the sting out of her words. "He's eager for you to go to New York and take your rightful place in polite society." Beatrice could hear the echoes of her father's voice in her mother's words. It was an old argument, and one that wasn't going away any time soon.

"I promise I'll be home in plenty of time." Beatrice avoided responding to Mama's statement. "Thank you! For everything." Her mother wouldn't speak of Beatrice's outing to her father unless she must, so she would do everything possible to honor that trust.

Beatrice took Princess through the back gate. If she rode across the town green, either Papa would see her riding or someone would comment on it. Perhaps Mrs. Dixon, the storekeeper's wife. She had clear ideas about what constituted proper behavior for young ladies. Beatrice's flower garden qualified. Her trips into the meadows and forests in search of unusual plantings did not. Why, when one complemented the other and both reflected the hands of the Creator, Beatrice had never figured out.

As soon as she had reached the spot where the road headed through the woods to the bridge crossing Bumblebee River, she let Princess have her head, and they galloped at a brisk pace. Half an hour there, half an hour back. . .that left her an hour to spend with her dear friend. Their friendship had been simpler in the days when they both went to school and needed no excuse to see each other on a daily basis. Of course, Papa had been gentler in those days, too, before he made all his money that had half the town jealous of him and the other half suspicious of where he had come up with all that cash. They accused him of profiteering, when good men were dying in defense of their country.

Beatrice shook off her worries. The Reids had always welcomed her, and today would be no exception. She might even see Peggy's Tuttle cousins. Perhaps she could exchange more than a simple *hello* with Calvin, the best man in the family in her opinion. When she reached the river bank, she reined Princess in to check the bridge. Were the dark splotches simply from melted snow, or were the planks slick with ice? She dismounted. A couple of tentative steps confirmed the bridge's firm footing. Leading Princess behind her, she walked forward a few steps at a time, avoiding the wet spots where possible.

Something flashed past Beatrice's shoulder and splashed in

the water. A female mallard landed and began paddling in the swift-flowing water. A second bird followed, passing within a few feet of Princess's head. The horse snorted and backed up. Her movement threw Beatrice off balance. Her foot found an icy patch, and she fell backward, landing on her rump.

For a stunned moment, Beatrice sat on the bridge, unmoving. Princess bent over and nudged her with her nose. Beatrice moved her right arm, then her left, and wiggled both legs. Everything appeared to be in working order. Around her, the bridge felt slick, and she didn't dare try to stand. Rising to her knees, she crawled forward inches at a time, seeking a safe place to stand. Her lovely coat would be filthy. Perhaps she should turn around straightaway and return home. But Mama would be furious whether she returned early or late, and she still hadn't seen Peggy. She would go ahead to the house.

"Did you lose something on the bridge?"

Beatrice looked up from her unladylike position on the bridge. Calvin Tuttle, Peggy's cousin. Of all the people to find her in this situation. . . Princess whinnied a greeting.

The wood beneath her felt dry, and Beatrice stood with the help of Princess's bridle. "I. . .took a little tumble." She knew her nose was as high in the air as Papa's ever was, but a girl had her pride.

"Oh, Bea."

Bea. Only Calvin Tuttle had ever called her that. Once, back in her first years of school, he had sent her a Valentine's card that read, "Will you bea mine?" That had started it, all those years ago. He'd teased her unmercifully, at least until the day she'd wished he'd notice her. By then, he saw her only as his younger cousin's friend and, as such, too young for his attention.

"Let me help you." Calvin closed the distance between them. He looked her over from head to toe. Probably checking to make sure she wasn't injured, but she felt her cheeks glow warm against the breeze that blew across the water. "You're not hurt?"

"Only my pride." She returned his gaze. Since he had returned from fighting in the recent war, their paths had not often crossed. They saw each other at church and at the occasional young people's frolic, but most days, he buried himself away at his farm. Papa had talked about it, how those Reids and Tuttles were building another farm west of the river, and whether or not it was a good idea. For herself, she thought it was industrious of Calvin.

"That bridge is slick. Let me help you over those last few steps." He walked onto the planks, the cleats of his boots sounding as sure as ice picks. When he reached her, he tucked her arm beneath his elbow.

She looked up into bright brown eyes. Oh my, Calvin had turned into a fine man. Always handsome, the last few years had only improved his appearance. His shoulders looked broader underneath his winter coat. His dark brown hair settled, a little long, over the collar to his jacket, and the smile in his eyes warmed her to her toes.

"Thank you very kindly." Her voice sounded breathy.

As she walked the last few steps across the bridge and onto the road on the far side of the river, the horse following behind her, her insides quivered like jelly.

No matter what Mama or Papa might say about today, she was mighty glad she had come.

two

Not many women of Calvin's acquaintance could manage to look ladylike and demure when crawling on their hands and knees. But somehow Beatrice Bailey managed it. She looked up at him with her doe-brown eyes, and he went all weak in the knees. The way she accepted his arm when he offered it made him feel like he was the Prince Regent of England escorting a fine lady to a ball, not a humble farmer helping a woman he'd known since she was a girl in pigtails. Back then, he'd called her "Bea" because of the way she buzzed around the classroom, curious about everything, butting her head in everywhere it didn't belong.

But now Beatrice was a grown woman, a *beautiful* woman, and the old teasing words stuck in his throat. He couldn't believe he had let the old nickname slip from his lips moments before. The creature standing before him was "Miss Bailey," and he'd better remember it.

Her mare cozied up to Bea and nuzzled her. "I'm fine, Princess." She reached into her pocket and held out a carrot with her gloved hands. *Princess.* So the Baileys treated even their horses like royalty. The mare was a beauty, no doubt about it, and of a sweet disposition like her mistress.

Bea took hold of the saddle and glanced over her shoulder at Calvin. "Would you mind turning your back?" Her voice held a hint of both imperious demand and nervous embarrassment.

"No need." He could have kicked himself for not thinking of her predicament sooner. "Let me assist you." He put his hands on her waist and lifted her into the saddle. The glimpse he caught of white petticoats, ruffles, and woolen stockings brought a blush to his cheeks. Why, he wasn't sure. He had assisted many ladies, not all family, onto the back of a horse, but none of them affected him the way Bea Bailey had.

Overhead, sparrows sang as if in celebration of the event. Apparently, even the birds of the forest agreed that Bea was pretty enough to inspire a song. His hands lingered on her waist a moment longer than necessary.

"Thank you."

Bea's voice broke his concentration, and he stepped away, his mind scrambling for something to say. "Are you headed for the Reids?"

She nodded. "For Peggy's birthday. I wouldn't miss it for all the world." She looked at her bedraggled dress. "Although I'm ashamed to show up like this. But I must dry out, and Peggy will see the humor of my adventure. Mama would keep me home for a week and call me irresponsible."

"Perhaps she should." *If you were in my care, I would do anything in my power to keep you safe.*

She looked at him as if he had said something offensive. "Why, Calvin Tuttle, would you keep me in a cage?"

A picture of her in a cage, wings fluttering against the bars, struck his imagination. *No, you should join your song to that of the birds in the sky. Fly alone, solo, to the heights of the heavens.* But no man would speak such sweet words to a woman unless. . . He shook his head. "I'm sorry. I spoke out of turn. I thought only of your safety."

She laughed, her pretty, even teeth flashing at him. "You're forgiven." She lifted the reins and urged Princess forward. "You are going to the celebration as well, of course?"

He nodded and walked alongside the horse. "We'd best make haste, or else the cake will be all gone before we get there." He stroked Princess's side. "But don't slow down on my account. Go on ahead and let them know I'm on my way."

Bea looked down at Calvin, her face unreadable. "I would rather walk with you." She shrugged her shoulders. "But if I want to avoid any ill effects from my fall, I'd best get warm and dry as soon as possible." Bending down, she spoke in a low voice. "Promise me we'll talk again later?"

"When we have opportunity."

Beatrice pressed her legs into the mare's sides, and she increased her pace. Calvin watched horse and rider heading down the road ahead of him, his throat dry in spite of the moisture permeating the air and ground around him.

❧

Beatrice resisted the urge to glance over her shoulder at Calvin. She hadn't seen much of the farmer in recent weeks. She had spotted him at church, where her parents kept her ensconced between them and away from any glances the young men of Maple Notch might send her way. She knew they did; no woman remained unaware of masculine attention, but so far none had dared come before her father. Perhaps they all knew Papa had determined only someone from New York, say a banker or a lawyer, would be worthy of his daughter. Someone ready to take over his business. Certainly not the son of a farmer.

So today's encounter felt almost God-ordained, one unplanned by either party. She had known she might see Calvin at Peggy's birthday celebration. But not like this, the two of them alone together.

A breeze stirred her clothes, and she shivered. Ahead she could see smoke spiraling from a chimney, announcing the proximity of the Reids' home. She urged Princess to a trot and entered the clearing.

Half a dozen horses were hitched to the railing in front of the cabin. Too many for the family; besides, they would walk, not ride the short distance between their farms. Princess whinnied and sped to reach the others. One of the horses neighed in response and turned his head.

A white star blazed down the forehead of a bay gelding. She recognized the markings. *Duke.* Before she had opportunity to process the implications, the door swung open.

"Beatrice Alice Bailey, what you are doing here?"

Papa.

She gulped. "I came to celebrate Peggy's birthday." Would Papa notice the state of her dress?

"That explains it." He accepted her unexpected presence with surprising ease.

"Welcome, Beatrice! Peggy will be so glad you came." Mrs. Reid came to her rescue. "Adam, come, help Miss Bailey down from her horse."

Beatrice hopped down onto a relatively dry patch of grass by the door. Her muddy cloak swept across Adam's legs, and he hesitated. Heat rushed into her cheeks, and she sped into the house, hoping Papa wouldn't notice.

He followed her in, and she held her breath. But he focused on the group gathered in the main room. In addition to family members, several other farmers from Maple Notch had gathered.

Before Beatrice could figure out what was going on, Peggy

beckoned to join her in a partitioned-off area at the back of the cabin. Beatrice sped to join her, hoping her friend had a way to repair the damage to her clothing.

"Dear friend." Peggy hugged Beatrice. "I didn't think you could make it after last night's snowfall!" She glanced at Papa. "Especially when Mr. Bailey didn't mention you were coming."

"I didn't decide to come until after he had left for work." Beatrice checked to make sure no one could hear and lowered her voice. "And there's worse. I fell on the bridge and—"

"Did you hurt yourself?" Peggy's hand flew to her mouth.

"No." True, tomorrow black-and-blue places might appear, but no serious damage had been done. "But my clothes are a different matter." She took off her cloak and for the first time examined the damage. Mud and splinters spattered along a dark stain down the back. The hem drooped from a small rip. She turned the cloak over to check the inside. Only one small spot had soaked through. She ran her hand down the length of her gown and found a tiny spot, no bigger than a two-bit piece. Relief flooded through her. "Oh, that's not so bad."

Peggy had left the room and returned with a cup of tea. She studied the cloak. "You won't want your father to know what happened." The two girls shared a conspiratorial look and giggled. "We can brush out the worst of it, and I've got needle and thread to fix the hem." Her voice sounded uncertain. "My pa wouldn't notice, but will yours?"

"It depends." Beatrice chewed her lip. "Do you know what's going on?" She giggled. "Unless all the families in Maple Notch have gathered to celebrate your nineteenth birthday. What's the name of the young man Calvin brought home?"

"Tobias Heath."

"Tobias. That must be it. He's of marriageable age, and he came."

"Stop that!" Peggy colored. "Everyone knows he's heart-broken over his sweetheart, who died during the war." She brought her hand to her mouth as if to hide a giggle. "Unless you fancy him yourself."

"The thought never entered my mind." Besides, dark curls and bright brown eyes came to Beatrice's mind when she thought of suitors. Not Tobias's pale looks.

"Of course not. Mr. Bailey won't let one of those gentlemen so much as look at you as long as he's present."

Beatrice heard the compassion beneath her friend's words. The thought made her sad, and she missed getting the thread in the needle.

"You do fancy someone. I knew it. Who?" Peggy's voice rose playfully.

"Shh." Beatrice felt heat rush into her cheeks, but blamed it on Papa's close presence. She dropped her voice to a whisper. "Not when *he's* here. You never answered my question." Perhaps she could distract Peggy's attention. "Why is everyone here?"

"Mr. Bailey came by this morning and asked if local farmers could meet today. Just my luck that it happened on my birthday." She shrugged.

They heard the rattle of the cabin door, and Beatrice peeked to see who had arrived. Calvin. Her heart sped up, and she realized she had held her breath. She took a sip of tea to cover her nervousness. Emptying the cup, she stood up.

"Let me get you another cup." Peggy stood to her feet.

"I can do it while you work on my cloak. Your stitches are better than mine. Thanks." She flashed a smile at Peggy and went to the spot where the teapot sat on the table.

Mr. Reid had greeted Calvin and led him to a seat by the window, facing away from the fireplace. The walk had reddened his cheeks, and the curls on his head sprang up like wildflowers. He exchanged a few words with his brother Solomon. The low murmurs of conversation seemed a bit tense. She poured the tea and carried her cup back into the bedroom.

"Girls?" Mrs. Reid came into the room, and Peggy folded over the offending cloak. "Are you ready to help me serve refreshments to our guests?"

"Of course." Beatrice was eager to hear what the meeting was about. "We already have tea steeping."

"That's good. Peggy dear, I'm afraid all I have to offer them is the cake we intended for your birthday."

"Of course we should share it. We're fortunate that we have it available." Peggy winked. "I'll cut a small piece for myself as well." She smoothed down her dress, and the two girls followed Mrs. Reid into the main room.

About twenty men had gathered in the cramped cabin. What would Mrs. Reid do for cups? Mama, known for setting the finest table in Maple Notch, only had place settings for fifteen, no more.

Peggy knew where to look. She reached onto a shelf over the work table and into cabinets, pulling out tankards and mugs and cups of every description. Mrs. Reid dug out a stack of platters. Of course, they served groups almost as large as this whenever their families gathered together.

Beatrice saw the cake, plum with a rich rum sauce, and her stomach rumbled. Breakfast seemed a long time ago. She spotted a wheel of cheese and decided to ask for a piece after they had served the guests. The *other* guests.

Peggy brought the first cup of tea to Papa, and Beatrice mouthed "thank you" to her friend. She moved silently among the others, tapping Calvin on the back and handing him tea. He tipped the cup to her in appreciation, and she smiled in return.

At that moment, Papa looked up and frowned in her direction but returned his attention to the gathering. "You must be wondering why I have called this meeting today."

Beatrice poured boiling water over fresh tea leaves to brew a second pot for the men.

❧

Yes, I do wonder why you asked us here. What with rescuing Beatrice from her tumble on the bridge, Calvin had forgotten about the meeting Hiram Bailey had called for the farmers.

"I am grateful you all made it here safely, with the bad weather we've been having." Bailey spoke with every appearance of sincerity. "But I thought the weather provided an opportunity for us to meet, since you won't be out in your fields working."

A low grumble greeted that remark. Last night's storm had struck a blow to more people than Calvin. He caught sight of Beatrice giving Tobias a mug of tea. She looked so natural, so gracious, as if this was her home and she the mistress. Had she known her father was coming? He doubted it. Bailey didn't seem the sort to appreciate his daughter interfering in his business affairs.

"This winter that is hanging on for an unseasonably long time is the reason for this meeting. I know that after last night's frost, many of you will need to replant. My daughter reminded me of that this morning, when she asked for more seed." He nodded in Beatrice's direction, and she looked up, a startled expression in her eyes.

Seed? What kind of seed did Beatrice need? She wasn't a farmer, but maybe they kept a kitchen garden or even flowers. She always brought unusual flowers and plants to school.

"And so you see. . ." Mr. Bailey had said something. *What?* How foolish of him to let his attention wander. Thinking about Beatrice, of all things, even if she did have a sweet smile and kind nature. He lifted his eyes to the banker and gave him his full attention.

"I know this is a difficult time for all of us here in Maple Notch."

How did the prolonged winter make business difficult for the banker? He didn't have to worry about whether another frost would kill his crops or if he would have a harvest come fall.

"I thought we could meet, neighbor to neighbor, to discuss our options."

Calvin thought he heard a snort. Beside him, Tobias hid his face in his mug.

"I don't see there's a problem, Hiram," Frisk, another Maple Notch oldtimer who had seen more winters come and go than most of them, said. "We'll plant a new crop, soon's the ground's thawed out a bit. It's nothing we ain't seen before." He fidgeted on his seat. "Iffen that's all you got to say, I got farm work that needs doin'." Others nodded their heads in agreement.

"How are you set for seed?" The banker glanced again at Beatrice. "As I said, my daughter's question brought it to mind."

"Why? You got some for sale down at your bank?" That

question came from Whitson, known for his quick wit and even quicker temper.

"Now, Seth," Micah Dixon, the storekeeper, said. "He's asked a valid question. I've laid in a store of extra seed at the emporium, if anyone needs to buy."

What you'd expect the storekeeper to say. If the farmers needed extra seed or money to purchase it, Dixon and Bailey would profit.

Beatrice circled by again and refilled Calvin's cup. She smiled at him. How could her features, which resembled her father's, be so appealing, and his, so prideful?

"I wanted to let you know that I'm here to help." Bailey spoke in a voice that sounded too loud for the cramped room. "Anything I can do. If you need something to help tide you over a rough patch, come on down to the bank."

"In exchange for a chunk of the crop, I expect." Uncle Stephen clapped Bailey on the shoulder. He shrugged and offered a gentle smile.

"We can't give away money; you know that, Mr. Reid. But I guarantee I'd give you fair terms. Can't say any better than that."

"I'm sure you will, Mr. Bailey. But Lord willing, I hope not to take advantage of your generous offer."

Calvin knew his uncle well enough to hear the tongue-in-cheek tone behind his comment. As for Calvin, he already owed money to the bank. He *had* to find a way to make this crop grow.

One way or another.

&

Papa had said some interesting things today. He was fond of saying money didn't grow on trees and other such nonsense, as if she didn't know that. So he hoped to lend money to farmers in need because of the hardship caused by weather conditions. She didn't know how that made her feel.

Well, they had to get money from somewhere, didn't they? Since banks were needed, why not Papa? Even though his true intentions were kind, he sounded a bit like King Midas, who wanted to make gold from everything he touched. After his speech, he conversed with Mr. Whitson. Her eyes scanned the room, checking for Calvin. Of course he would stay for Peggy's birthday celebration.

She looked at the pan that had held the birthday cake, all gone but for crumbs. She resisted the urge to dip her fingers in the pan and gather a few for herself. Behind her, someone giggled, and she turned.

Peggy had a tiny piece on a plate. "You should have kept a piece for yourself. No one would have minded. That's what I did." She took a delicate bite in her mouth and pretended to swoon with pleasure at the flavor.

"Of course. It's *your* birthday." Beatrice smiled at her friend.

"Are you staying for the party?" Calvin appeared at her elbow.

She looked up, all the way up, into those eyes the color of the rich earth when it had been turned for planting, deep and dark and brown.

"What party?" Peggy had finished her cake and brushed the crumbs into the dustpan. "The cake's gone."

"You haven't opened your presents yet." Calvin reached into his coat and pulled out a package wrapped in plain brown paper. Peggy reached for it, and he twisted away, bumping into Beatrice in the narrow confines of the kitchen.

"My apologies." But his grin gave lie to his words. He lowered his voice. "Were you able to make repairs to your cloak?"

She wiggled her hand in a manner indicating yes and no. "Can I see the present?" She held out her hands for the package, and he handed it to her.

"Hmm. Nothing obvious, like a book." She held it up to her ear and shook it. A slight clinking reached her ears, but not from a bell or a chain. "I can't tell. You'll have to open it to see." She gave it to Peggy instead of back to Calvin.

"Not fair!" He protested.

"Beatrice." Papa's voice interrupted the good-natured teasing. Momentarily, she had forgotten that the piper would call his tune and expect her attendance at any minute.

"It's time to go, daughter." His voice, although pleasant enough, brooked no alternative.

"I brought a gift for Peggy's birthday. May I stay?"

"I'll be happy to see her safely home, sir," Calvin said.

"That won't be necessary." Papa used his King Midas voice again. "Go get the gift, and then we'll be on our way."

"Yes, Papa." Beatrice walked into the bedroom. Behind his back, Peggy pouted, then grinned, letting her know she harbored no hard feelings. Shaking out the cloak, Beatrice decided one wouldn't notice the dirt unless one looked closely. She extracted her present, a bottle of scented Florida water she knew Peggy liked, and returned to the living room with dragging steps.

Beatrice handed the package to her friend and hugged her. "I'm sorry I can't stay."

"Another time," Peggy promised.

Without volition, Beatrice's eyes sought out Calvin. Another time, *he* wouldn't be there.

She didn't know why that thought made her sad.

three

Calvin shivered inside his cabin. By the summer solstice, he expected the advanced season to make a hearth fire unnecessary overnight. But as his feet slammed onto the cold planks of his floor and he pulled his shirt tight around his chest, he regretted the lack of warmth.

By the time he shrugged into his work shirt and breeches, Tobias had already started a small fire. "Thought you said it wouldn't get cold last night."

"It shouldn't have." Calvin's voice was low enough to register as a mumble. He wasn't sure if Tobias could hear, or if he even wanted him to hear the discouragement in his voice.

"Maybe not."

So Tobias had heard.

"But take a look outside." Tobias jutted his chin in the direction of the window.

Calvin approached it slowly. As he feared, a world of white covered the ground yet again. Snow enchanted and delighted in October, signaling winter's stark beauty and a season of rest ahead. In March and April, heavy snowfall had signaled winter's last hurrah before the land sprang to life again. It promised adequate snowmelt to water crops during the summer months. By May, snow was unwelcome, and in June, unheard of. Would it even snow at the height of summer, in July?

Calvin blew against the window as if by that action he

could disprove the evidence of his feet and his eyes, and that instead of unseasonable cold, summer reigned with its temperate climate. But the place where his mouth had touched the pane formed a circle of droplets. He shook his head. Yet another crop dead in the fields. Good thing he had held some seed back in May, in fear snow would fall again.

He dug his woolen socks out of the darning basket and pulled his boots from underneath his bed. A storage box held his winter things once he expected nothing worse than muddy fields over the next few months.

"Hey, have a biscuit and some coffee before you head out in that cold." Tobias plunked down a couple of plates on the table. "I'm not going out there until I get something warm in my stomach."

"City boy." Calvin accompanied this grumble with a smile and joined Tobias at the table. They wolfed down the grub in a matter of minutes and headed for the fields. On the way, Calvin glanced at the barn, where he had placed the yoke in hopes of borrowing Solomon's ox. If the fair weather had continued, he'd intended to clear more of his field. Not now. He pulled on mittens and a hat and headed for the clearing.

He walked up one row and down another until he reached the stump of an oak tree that looked as though it had been there since before the first white man had arrived in the New World. He had made a wide berth around the tree when he scattered seeds. Anything planted in the neighborhood of the tree roots got suffocated in their extensive, underground system.

But when he looked by the old stump, he had a thought. Could he make the tree's root system work for him? He had to find some answers. When May ended without more snowfall, he had breathed a sigh of relief. Who would have expected it on the twenty-first of June? Had Bea planted new seed as she planned, hoping it would grow? If so, she faced disappointment as well.

Rubbing his chin, he pondered the stumps of oak, maple, and elm trees scattered across his field. The thought process diverted his attention while he walked up and down the rows, confirming that once again, frost and snow had killed the seedlings. Would the stand of trees crowding the edge of the fields provide cover if he planted close by? Could they shield the plants from more snowfall or insulate them? He shook his head. Anything he planted there would compete with all the bounty of God's creation for the earth's nutrients, or provide food for wild creatures. He might harvest a small amount, but not enough to hold off the bank's foreclosure.

He began the painful process of turning under the plants, churning ideas as he did so. An answer eluded him, but he would find it eventually.

❧

Beatrice looked at the cotton dress with a pattern of lilac sprigs she had planned to wear in celebration of the first day of summer. Sighing, she hung it in her armoire and settled for her dark green linsey-woolsey dress. The garment was serviceable, even pretty. But she tired of wearing it after the unrelenting coolness of the year.

Early this morning, Papa had left the house, his face set in stern lines. Had he called another meeting of the farmers at the Reids? She considered running after him, asking about his plans, and begging to go along to visit with Peggy if that happened. But she didn't. He would only refuse.

Beatrice brightened. At least the snow would delay her

departure for New York, where her parents hoped to spend Independence Day. Did she dare hope they would cancel the trip altogether? If she didn't go this year, perhaps Papa would let go of this foolish notion of her marrying some city fellow, when she could imagine nothing better than to settle down with one of the men of Maple Notch.

Calvin Tuttle's face swam into her mind, and she felt heat rush to her cheeks, thankful no one could see. She took a seat by the small fire Bessie Angus, Cook's helper and Beatrice's maid, had started earlier. Her Bible opened to the pressed lilacs she had rescued during last month's snowfall. Today's Bible reading took Beatrice to the Song of Solomon. Some of the things Solomon said made her blush, and she wouldn't ask for an explanation, not even of Mama. But other things, like the beautiful description of springtime, made her spirit sing. Even this year when summer never seemed to come, she listened to the chatter of birds outside her window and hoped with them for a break in the weather. Her cat Patches enjoyed it, too, watching them and striking at the pane with her paws from time to time.

But this morning, the birds remained quiet, at least too quiet to hear through the heavy glass. Over the town green, geese flew in lazy circles. Did they feel as trapped as she did? With another day indoors, Mama would insist she spend the hours stitching on the napkins, tablecloths, and other linens for her hope chest. In a word, *boring*. She already had enough, given to her by Great-grandmother Bailey, for a family of twelve. She, who didn't even have a husband yet, nor the prospect of one. The thought made her giggle. Who was the special someone God had in mind for her?

"Beatrice." Mama's voice floated up the stairs.

Beatrice flexed her fingers and sighed. "Yes, Mama?"

"When are you coming down, dear? The sun's been up for hours. As Ben Franklin said, 'No morning sun lasts a whole day.'"

"I'm ready now." Beatrice closed her Bible and set it on the table by the window. She looked across the green and caught sight of a group of men making their way to the church. Maybe Papa *had* called a meeting today, at the meetinghouse.

One of the men looked up, and she caught a clear view of the dark hair framing his sun-kissed face and brown eyes. Calvin. He lifted his hand to his eyebrow as if to salute. Then he turned his head and laughed at something one of the others had said.

Beatrice decided to attend the men's meeting.

❧

Calvin thought he had glimpsed Beatrice in the second-floor window of her parents' house. It sat on the edge of the town green, proclaiming itself the finest in Maple Notch and even better than most of what Burlington had to offer.

"Sounds like Hiram Bailey wants to make a second fortune." Solomon shook his head. "Whatever the man needs all that money for is beyond me."

"Ma says Mrs. Bailey goes to Burlington to shop," Adam said. "Dixon's Emporium isn't good enough for her."

We're as bad as a bunch of old biddies. Calvin thought of Bea's face and bit back a smile. *If I had someone as fine as Bea to buy for, why, I'd give her everything in my power.* He looked again at the window, but she was gone. Maybe he'd seen a pine branch waving its snow-laden limbs in front of the window.

"That's enough," Uncle Stephen said. "He's doing honest business."

"Which is more than we can say for his conduct during the war." Solomon huffed.

"None of which was proven," their uncle reminded them. "We're almost there. And we've all agreed to hear the man out." He nudged Solomon in the ribs. "Besides, some would say the Tuttles have no call to talk against him, since your grandfather was a Tory sympathizer."

Solomon bristled, as Uncle Stephen surely had known he would. Did he do it on purpose? To divert attention from gossiping about Mr. Bailey?

"He who is without sin can cast the first stone—is that what you're suggesting?" Calvin asked.

"I'm saying, listen without judging him ahead of time. Let the past stay in the past."

"Amen." Tobias murmured.

Was he thinking about his painful past and the losses he had sustained? His smile removed Calvin's doubts. He suspected they were both thinking of the plan they had concocted when they toured the field that morning. What would the other farmers think of it?

Much the same group gathered at the meetinghouse as had come to Uncle Stephen's home last month. The men sat on benches across the front of the church, where daylight streamed through the windows, providing natural light. The sun shone so brightly it was hard to believe it had snowed only last night, or that the air was crisp and cool and free of the insects that usually plagued Vermont by this time of year. In spite of the four walls and the fire burning in a small wood stove, the air remained a cold reminder of the night's disaster.

The Reid and Tuttle men, with Tobias, took up one entire bench. When everyone had settled, Pastor Cabot walked to the pulpit. "Good morning, gentlemen. As always, I am glad to see you in the Lord's house, but I regret the circumstances." He spoke in his solemn voice, the same one he used whether describing the Lord's glory or the death of a saint. The tone said, "Listen up. This is important."

Calvin settled down. The parson's sermons could take awhile. He focused his gaze on a picture of Christ praying in the garden that hung behind the preacher at the front of the church. Times like this, he felt a bit like Peter, James, and John, who couldn't stay awake to pray with Jesus for an hour. Everyone agreed that prayer and the preaching of the Word were important, but sometimes Calvin's mind tended to wander. All it took was a sound like the creaking of the church door. He twisted his head to see who was coming in before he thought about it. Silhouetted against the cold sunshine pouring in with the rush of cold air stood a feminine form, with sunshine gleaming on her golden hair.

Bea Bailey. With her entrance, the air in the church warmed by about twenty degrees. Calvin forced himself to look forward, where Pastor Cabot had paused in mid-sentence but didn't comment on Bea's arrival.

"And so, brethren, it appears God has decided to visit us with a season of snow. A year without a summer, in fact."

The Year of No Summer. The *Farmer's Almanac* hadn't seen this one coming.

"It's only June," Whitson quipped, and nervous laughter broke out across the congregation.

Cabot managed a thin smile in recognition of the witticism. "Brother Bailey suggested we gather together to beseech the Lord's favor for seasonable weather through the remaining summer months and, if it be His will, to even delay fall's arrival until we have a full harvest. This church is a house of prayer, and I am always glad to open our doors for that purpose."

So Calvin's earlier rambling thoughts about the disciples in the Garden of Gethsemane had hit close to the mark. This *was* a prayer meeting. He stole a glance around at the men gathered. Some shuffled their feet; others stared at the floor. Old man Frisk had his hands tucked under his armpits as if to keep them warm. Tobias stared straight ahead, focused on the planks lining the back wall of the meetinghouse. Perhaps he was counting the boards or the knotholes. Calvin had done that many times as a child.

"That's all fine and good, Parson, but I for one would like to know what people plan on doing about the blight on the year. Does anyone have any ideas?" Frisk had dropped his hands to his sides and stood up.

Frisk voiced Calvin's thoughts. He suspected most of the men present were asking themselves the same question.

"I've already asked my wife to use our food sparingly. But no one expected this in time to set aside from last year's harvest."

"Men." Bailey stood to his feet. "I appreciate your concerns. But you have my assurance that no one in Maple Notch will go hungry because of the weather."

No, we'll just all be in debt to you. Calvin didn't voice the thought.

"But perhaps as Parson Cabot says, if we repent and seek the Lord's face, He will turn this disaster away from us."

At that, Whitson jumped to his feet. His face as red as a maple leaf in autumn, he said, "If anyone needs to repent, it's *you*, Mr. Bailey. Profiting from the sale of potash across the border during the war. The *illegal* sale."

Tobias's head jerked up at that. Calvin mouthed *later*. The banker wasn't the only Vermonter to make good money from the thriving potash trade during the embargo of trade with Britain. What turned the folks of Maple Notch against him was the way he continued to smuggle the wood ashes—useful for everything from making soap to tanning hides—into Canada during the war. They saw it as helping the enemy.

"Mr. Whitson, there is no need to insult me. I only seek to face a common problem together."

"The way you faced the British?" Frisk spoke now. "We didn't trust you then, and we don't see any reason to trust you now."

Calvin heard feet tapping the floor behind him. Bea. What must she be thinking, feeling, as the men of the town attacked her father? Without further thought, he jumped to his feet.

"I have something to say."

His entrance into the fray surprised the others into silence.

"Yes, Mr. Tuttle?" The preacher invited him to speak.

Calvin turned in a circle, looking at the people gathered in the room. Tobias winked at him and nodded. Bea looked at him, her eyes seas of frothy water. At least Whitson had settled back on the bench.

"Speak up, man." Bailey sounded relieved someone had interrupted the fracas. "I'm sure we're all anxious to hear any insights you have into this situation."

Calvin reviewed the proposal that he and Tobias had formed yesterday. It seemed so simple, he wondered why others hadn't tried it.

"I have an idea for a way to keep the ground warm when. . . if. . .another cold spell hits. I had planned on pulling out the tree stumps left in my field this summer, but this inclement weather has thrown all my plans off." He brushed his hand across his forehead, pushing his hair back. "So yesterday I was thinking about how the tree roots tangle up my plants and wondered, why not make that work *for* me? Instead of yanking them out with a pair of oxen, I'll burn them out."

"We all know how to do that. That's nothing new." Frisk voiced what others probably were thinking.

"I know. It's a slow, smoky process. That's why most of the time we do something else. But I thought, if the roots are burning, it will help keep the soil warm. Warm enough to withstand a day or two of snowfall, at least."

Blank looks answered his idea. At last Solomon cleared his throat. "That's an interesting idea, for sure, but it seems to me more likely that snow would put out the fire."

"Even if your idea works, it won't help those of us with older farms where we've already cleared out those tree stumps." At least Frisk put his disapproval in kind words.

No one else spoke. Maybe Calvin's great idea wouldn't work after all. Before he sat down, he noticed Bea smiling at him, a thoughtful expression on her face. She nodded in his direction.

Why did her approval warm his heart? What did *she* know about farming?

four

Beatrice couldn't believe the other farmers had dismissed Calvin's brilliant idea with hardly a word. Could she adapt it to her own garden?

She was considering leaving before her father commented on her presence, when Parson Cabot stood up again. "We will coordinate distributions for those in need here at the church. Anyone wishing to donate or anyone in need, please contact me privately."

Beatrice decided to stay and talk with him after the conclusion of the meeting; Papa would approve of her desire to help those less well off than they were.

The preacher closed in prayer, and the men prepared to leave.

"Heating the ground from the roots up. That's an entertaining notion." Mr. Reid clapped Calvin on the back. A dull red crept into his cheeks.

"I don't know." Frisk joined in the bantering. "It's better than waiting for snow to kill the next planting."

"Anything's better than that." Whitson chuckled. "Unless it's a keg and a chair by the fire to keep me warm." He glanced in Beatrice's direction. "Not that you folks know anything about that."

"Maybe you're just jealous." Beatrice's heart warmed when Solomon spoke in his brother's behalf. "You don't have any stumps left to burn." He gestured to the door. "Let's be on our way."

Beatrice stood when they passed her bench, wanting to speak a word of encouragement to Calvin, but not daring to be so forward. She didn't have to worry. He paused while the others went on.

"I'm glad you're here today." The red had left his cheeks. "Peggy loves the fragrance you gave her for her birthday. When I go to their cabin, I feel like I've walked into a Paris salon."

"Tell her I'm glad she's enjoying it. Mama recommended it." She lowered her voice. "I think your idea is brilliant. I'm going to see if I can adapt it for our kitchen garden."

He worked his lips. Perhaps she shouldn't have spoken. Like her father, he might think women shouldn't worry about such things. After a moment's pause, he said, "Thanks for the encouragement, Miss Bailey." He dipped his head and took his leave.

"Godspeed, Mr. Tuttle," she whispered after him. Then she shook herself. She didn't want Papa to catch her staring after Calvin Tuttle. Instead, she walked to the front of the sanctuary where Mr. Dixon and Papa were speaking with the preacher.

"Beatrice." Papa's voice held a note of caution. "Are you waiting for me to bring you home?"

"No, Papa. I wanted to offer my assistance in gathering goods to help people through this hard time." She smiled.

He opened his mouth, closed it. Before he could speak, Parson Cabot said, "I'm sure you will do an admirable job. Mrs. Cabot has already started making plans, but I'm certain she'll be glad of your assistance. She's scheduling a planning session for tomorrow afternoon, if you care to join the effort."

"She'll be there with Mrs. Bailey." Papa didn't give her a

chance to answer for herself, but at least he agreed to her participation. "We will take our leave of you then, Parson. Good day." He took Beatrice's arm and walked with her out the door.

"You don't need to walk home with me. 'Tis only around the corner of the green." Beatrice enjoyed the brisk air on her face, warmer now than in the early morning. Already the snow patches on the green were shrinking.

"It's my pleasure, Beatrice." To her surprise, Papa steered her in the opposite direction from the house. "This gives us a few quiet moments to talk."

In spite of the promised conversation, Papa didn't say anything for a short time, as he helped her avoid puddles forming in the street.

"Beware of becoming overly involved with the charity project." When he spoke at last, his words surprised her.

"Why? Aren't you always encouraging us to help others?"

"That's not it." They reached the bank and passed it in silence. "You will be leaving for New York once the roads are clear. I have made arrangements for you to stay with my mother for a time."

"But, Papa." *I don't want to go.*

"You will obey me in this. I am not comfortable with you mingling with the farmers and their families. We have higher hopes for you."

Doesn't what I want matter? Ultimately, no, it didn't. Beatrice swallowed her disappointment. "Yes, Papa. But. . . until then. . .I can plan on going to the parsonage tomorrow?"

Papa nodded his head. "Yes." He brought her to the door of their house and waited for her to enter before heading to the bank.

Calvin lagged behind, not wanting to endure his family's good-natured teasing. His ploy didn't work. Solomon trudged on ahead, anxious to get back to his home, but Uncle Stephen stayed behind with him and Tobias.

"Are you really planning to burn out the root systems?"

Calvin shrugged. "At the least, it will rid my fields of the stumps."

Uncle Stephen turned to Tobias. "What do you think of this idea?"

"It's not my farm, but I want to do it."

Good ol' Tobias, standing up for him.

They stopped by the fence, and his uncle jumped up on the crossed poles after clearing off the snow. The trees looked odd, snow coating the few green leaves that still hung on to the branches. Uncle Stephen hit the wood with the flat of his hand and surveyed the trees around him. "We always stopped by this very spot on Rogation Day, back when I was a boy. We no longer do that. It's a pity."

"Rogation Day. What's that?" Tobias asked.

"I suppose a town boy wouldn't know about that," Calvin said in a teasing voice. "Back before Maple Notch had a church, the circuit preacher came around to bless the new crops. Dad says there was a lot of good-natured bumping and pushing around the boundary markers, so they'd know where their parcel began and ended."

"That's right." Uncle Stephen nodded. "As I said, we always came this way. I knew every rock and tree. When I was a boy, there were a lot more trees here. We had cold winters, I suppose. I don't rightly remember. I had fun playing in the snow and helping Pa fix up the farm. Leastwise, until he died.

After we won our independence and my brother chose to move away. . .well, it seemed like nothing could separate me from this land." He brushed the rest of the snow off the fence and jumped down. "But now, I wonder."

Was his uncle considering moving away? He had heard rumors among the other farmers, but not in his family.

"Come on. Let's go." Uncle Stephen joined him, and they continued walking down the trail.

A few yards ahead, they reached the spot where their paths separated. "I'm praying for you, Calvin. One of the things I learned during the War for Independence was that God will make a way when it seems impossible. He did for us."

"Calvin's told me some of the stories." Tobias flashed a grin. "That his mother lived in a cave near their fields with her family when the Tories wanted to take over the Patriot land. How his father helped her, against the wishes of his grandfather."

"That's right." Uncle Stephen's mouth formed a thin smile that remembered a faraway time. "Don't be afraid to ask for help, Calvin. You've got family here."

Calvin strove to loosen his clenched teeth. How could he hope to ever make a home for himself. . .for a wife and a family. . .if he ran home when hard times came? But he knew the love behind the offer and refused to take offense. "Thanks."

❧

The following morning, Calvin and Tobias headed to the fields early. They spent the better part of the morning turning the ruined crop over and preparing the ground for yet another planting. At noon, they dug out the sandwiches they had made that morning.

Tobias sat down on the stump of a maple tree and propped

his knee on the weathered wood. "So how do we go about setting the roots to burning?"

"You're as bad as a little kid." Calvin responded with good humor. "I have to tell you everything."

"But you have to admit that I'm a fast learner. Good thing I'm humble, too. Good looking to boot." Tobias took a bite and chewed before adding with a sly grin, "Not that Miss Bailey would ever notice. She only has eyes for you."

Calvin's shoulders jerked in reaction to Tobias's unexpected comment. "Miss Bailey's father has noticed *both* of us, and we don't pass muster. Now let's get to work."

In spite of the warm air, Calvin built a fire. He would lay the auger in the center, to bring the end to a red-hot point before he would insert it into a tree stump. "Let's go back to the cabin. I'll return the hoes and get the auger. You go into the cabin and fill up the kettle with water and bring it on out. I'll grab the salt."

Tobias crooked an eyebrow at Calvin as though wondering about his sanity.

"You'll see." The snow had melted away since the storm, and once again, birds sang in the trees. Too bad he couldn't relax and enjoy it, search out the goslings that had left the nest not long before.

"Too bad you don't have two of those things." Tobias pointed to the auger as they returned to the field. "Not that I know much about it, but I could learn."

"We'll see what progress we make today. If I don't finish today, we'll ask Solomon if we can borrow his tomorrow. Today, you can watch and learn." He didn't mention that he needed practice himself since he hadn't burned tree stumps since he was a little boy.

After the water was heating over the fire and the auger prepared, Calvin touched its point to the center of the stump. The wood smoked as the auger hit it and charred through the surface. Calvin twisted the tool, making the hole wider and deeper. Once the opening was about half an inch across, he lifted the tool and checked the end. Still hot enough for a second hole.

He turned to where Tobias stood watching. "Now it's your turn. Pour salt into each hole as I make it."

Working as a team, the men repeated the process, pausing to reheat the auger once, creating a series of holes in a diagonal line crisscrossing the stump. "That's enough. Next we pour hot water into the holes. I brought the dipper."

Tobias stopped by the boiling kettle. "Why water? How can you burn something with water in it?"

"It decays faster." Calvin started on the next stump while Tobias filled the holes with water.

"I'm done," Tobias announced. He brought the salt to the stump where Calvin worked.

"Wait a minute." Calvin set down the auger, glad for a break. "Now we start the fire." He piled kindling and small branches on top of the stump Tobias had treated and lit them. "I still need to come up with something to make a chimney for the fire. Burns better that way."

Tobias looked across the field. "And we have to do this for every stump in your field?"

Calvin nodded. "We'll relight the fire every day. Normally we'd clean out the ash it leaves so it would burn faster, but I want to keep the ground warm as long as possible. Time enough to clean out the mess when we're sure the weather's going to stay warm."

Tobias whistled. "That's going to take us awhile. Let's get busy."

❧

" 'Tis hard to believe that we had snowfall here only two nights ago. Already the ground has dried," Mama said as she walked with Beatrice to the parsonage.

"Someone built a snowman on the green." Beatrice cocked her head to study the lopsided figure now melted to a lump not much taller than a child. "Must have been the parson's children." Here and there among the muddy morass of the town common, the ever hopeful grass poked short shoots into the air. The trees were in worse shape. She stopped to check the buds on her favorite oak that dominated the side by their house. She found a few fledgling leaves clinging to its branches, branches that by this time of year should be invisible under the foliage. But by and large, she couldn't even find any green emerging from the buds, promising the new year's growth had started.

"That snowman will be gone tomorrow if the weather continues warm as it is." Mama patted Beatrice's hand. "Since we're so far north, I'm sure the weather to the south has been more pleasant. We will have you in New York in time for Independence Day, have no fear." She slowed her steps as they approached the meetinghouse. "I was your age when I met your father. You are of an age when your thoughts naturally turn to marriage and motherhood."

Beatrice's cheeks pinked. Mama rarely spoke of such personal things.

"He came to New York on a business trip, and even then I saw the man he would become. You might not guess it now, but he was handsome and strong. I knew then he would be successful at whatever he turned his hand to."

"Did Grandfather Purcell object to you marrying someone from the north country?"

"Not for long. He could see Mr. Bailey's sterling qualities. And my mother helped persuade him." Mama looked quite pleased with herself. "And soon some young lad as fine as your father will be occupying your mind and heart."

Beatrice's thoughts strayed to Caleb, but she suppressed the image. Papa wouldn't entrust her future to someone who hoped an experimental stump burnout would save his crops—his livelihood.

Somehow, Papa had convinced Grandfather Purcell that he was worthy of her mother's hand in marriage. What would a local boy have to do to convince Papa of the same?

Mama patted Beatrice on the arm. "We'll leave on the next stagecoach that comes through Maple Notch." The look in her eye told Beatrice Mama couldn't wait to get to New York.

Beatrice looked at the shrinking snow patch and almost wished snow would fall another time, even after the advent of summer. Clear roads meant travel became possible.

"Ah! Here we are, at the parsonage."

Mrs. Cabot came to the door. "Come in! Lovely weather today, isn't it?" She took their coats and hats and gestured for them to find a seat. A handful of ladies had gathered. Peggy gave a tiny wave in Beatrice's direction, and her heart lifted.

Mama took her place in a cushioned rocking chair, the most comfortable seat in the room, as if it was hers by right. Mrs. Cabot hesitated before taking a chair by the kitchen. "This is a good seat. I can go in and out easily from here."

Her statement made Beatrice wonder if the parson's wife had been sitting in the chair Mama had claimed. She herself took a chair by Peggy.

"I believe we're all here now." Mrs. Cabot's smile welcomed all, from little Nellie Warner, too young to help in any meaningful way, to Mama, sitting in her chair like the queen of Maple Notch. "This year has been difficult for all of us, but especially for those who are farmers in our midst. So far every crop has failed, and if there is another freeze, there is little chance for harvest."

Beatrice's thoughts skittered to Calvin's plans to warm his fields. Would he succeed? She jerked her mind back to Mrs. Cabot's words.

"Mr. Cabot suggested we make preparations for the worst as a community. The church always sets some things aside for the needy, but our cupboards are almost bare. I fear things will get worse before they get better. I hoped that together we could suggest some means to meet the needs arising among us."

"I don't know about that." Mrs. Whitson, as quarrelsome as her husband was contentious, spoke. "Times like this tax all our resources. I don't have nothing left over to give away."

Beatrice harrumphed to herself. The Whitsons had one of the most successful farms in the valley. Papa had talked about the good business they brought the bank's way.

Murmurs of agreement spread across the room. "We want to help," Peggy said. "But we're not sure how to do it."

Beatrice waited for her mother to say something. They had resources, and their livelihood didn't depend directly on the whims of weather. But if the fields didn't produce, no amount of money could buy enough.

Beatrice thought back to the Bible stories she had read so often and spoke. "Perhaps we can learn a lesson from Joseph.

Of course, God didn't send any of us warning that we'd have this bad year, but couldn't we set aside some of what's left from last harvest? Collect it in a central place?"

"Like a tax?" Mrs. Whitson asked. "We already pay enough to the government."

"Think of it as an investment. In our community. A protection against next year."

"And who'd be in charge of it? You? Your father?"

Uneasy laughter rippled across the room.

"Of course not." Mama frowned at her.

Beatrice felt the need to defend her idea. "We could reassess the need next year. God willing, the farmers will have bumper crops next season. I thought knowing something was available if this year's crops fail might bring peace of mind."

Furrows appeared between Peggy's eyebrows, as if she were turning Beatrice's idea over in her mind. Her friend seemed uncertain of her plan, and that troubled her.

Mrs. Reid, Peggy's mother, spoke. "Beatrice, I'm sure your heart means well, but you're not a farmer. We plan for special circumstances such as this. Our families have been through troublesome harvests before, and will again. We'll weather the storm, you'll see, even if we have to make do without some things."

The women in the group murmured their agreement, and Beatrice knew they wouldn't heed her ideas. She struggled with her disappointment. Was she imagining problems where none existed? Was she only thinking of things as a banker might, in terms of profit and loss, not in terms of personal hopes and dreams?

A few minutes later, the meeting broke up with little progress beyond a verbal agreement to gather food if a need was expressed. Beatrice wished she could shake the unease that plagued her. Not everyone had families. And some without families wouldn't want to ask when others had more mouths to feed.

Someone like. . .Calvin.

Beatrice hoped it wouldn't come to that.

five

Before the church ladies could meet a second time, Mama announced a change of plans for Beatrice. One morning, Mama came into the room to look over the gowns that hung in the armoire. She pulled out a buttercup gown that had been fashioned for Beatrice last summer. "This will have to do."

Beatrice had worn the gown to Sunday meetings and a few other special festivities. Never during the middle of the week. "What's happening?"

"Your father has invited us to go with him to Burlington tomorrow. He asked that we dress in our best. I think that while we are in town, I shall buy fabric for some new gowns."

"But if we go to Burlington, we'll miss the church women's meeting."

Mama clucked. "They can manage without us this once, I fancy. Your father rarely takes us on his business trips."

Beatrice's heart went out to Mama. In truth, her few trips out of Maple Notch were always occasions for rejoicing, opportunities to visit with her sisters who remained in the larger town. Inside her portmanteau, Mama had packed only one gown. A dark blue morning dress lay on the coverlet for her traveling costume. Beatrice breathed a sigh of relief. Without more dressy garments, they couldn't be planning to ship her to New York.

"Mr. Bailey thought you might enjoy shopping for seeds.

Decide for yourself what you might want to plant in the garden."

Beatrice's heart sped up at the prospect. "Perhaps I can learn how others are combating the frosts the farmers are battling this year."

"No need to trouble your mind about that, dear." Mama stepped close and for a long moment, Beatrice feared she would pinch her cheeks to make them appear pink. But she didn't move her hands, and the look on her face reminded Beatrice of the day she saw a robin pushing her babies out of the nest. Was this, in fact, not a trip to Burlington but to New York? She glanced again at the scant items in her traveling bag. *No*, she decided.

Mama bent over the bag and rearranged the contents, tucking in Beatrice's Bible. "Perhaps we can make time to visit the booksellers while we are there. My sister Rose has mentioned a new book, *Waverley*, that you might enjoy."

Beatrice blinked at that. Mama rarely encouraged her to visit the bookshop and never to read such frivolous-sounding titles. "I'd like that." She kept her reservations to herself, lest Mama change her mind. "When are we leaving?"

"Later this morning. The roads are clear today, and Mr. Bailey wants to get as far as the ordinary at Milton by nightfall."

"But Mrs. Cabot—"

"I've already sent her a note. She'll understand."

A trip of a couple of days, with the promise of a new gown and more books. Beatrice warmed to the idea. What harm could she come to in such a short amount of time? In case they were delayed, she decided to write short notes to both Calvin and Peggy. "We shan't be gone long," she penned, then stuck the tip of the feather between her teeth, wondering what to say. She sent a prayer up to heaven. "I'll pray for good weather to hasten the growth of this year's crop and so we won't be stranded in Burlington. I long to return to Maple Notch before Independence Day."

৯

Calvin looked up to see Tobias leaning on his hoe, staring down the lane for the third time in an hour. "She won't get here any more quickly if you stare all day. Haven't you ever heard that a watched pot never boils?"

Tobias didn't pretend not to know what Calvin was talking about. He had been looking down the road to town for the ladies returning from church for the last hour. A single question to Calvin—*"Is anyone calling on your cousin Peggy?"*—was all it had taken to diagnose Tobias's interest. Glad as Calvin was to see his friend coming out of the grief-filled daze that had dulled his mind since his betrothed's death, he didn't think twice about the unfortunate inclinations of his own heart. Hiram Bailey would *never* consider a farmer good enough for his daughter.

Calvin decided to take mercy on his friend. "But it is past noon, and we've not yet eaten. Let's take our midday break. And pray the ladies come along while we're resting."

Tobias laughed and stretched his arms, causing the muscles to ripple across his back. Perhaps they should continue working. Peggy might take more notice of Tobias's honest labor and growing farm skills than of two men at their leisure. But if they did that, Calvin couldn't hide his own growing agitation about what news of Bea Peggy might bring.

He drank from the water dipper and allowed himself another ladle to sprinkle over his head to cool it down.

Looking across the sun-kissed field, he wouldn't believe snow had covered the ground only a couple of days ago unless he had seen it himself. Of course warmth from the smoking tree stumps added to the rays beating on their backs. He reached for their shirts and tossed one to Tobias. "We'd best get presentable."

The two of them stuffed their arms into sleeves and pulled the tops on. With the water he had dribbled over his head, Calvin felt as fresh as if he had just stepped out of the river. Tobias poured water over his hands and ran the hands through his hair, giving himself a similar look. Would the ladies think they had whiled the morning away?

"They'll know how hard we've been working when they see the corn mounds. . .if they can see through the smoke, that is."

Once again, Tobias appeared to have read Calvin's mind. He shook his head. Some of the smoke had darkened his shirt, so it did look a little work worn and not fresh from the laundry. The golden highlights the sun teased from Tobias's hair glittered with the water. "You'll set Peggy's heart aflutter, that's for certain." Calvin cut the cheese wedge in half and was handing it to his friend when they heard soft laughter beyond the copse of trees on the edge of the clearing. One thing about Calvin's land: it lay straight on the route from town to the Reid and Tuttle farms.

Peggy noticed them first and waved. Calvin expected her to have eyes only for Tobias, but instead she called, "Cousin! I have a letter for you."

"Beatrice." Tobias mouthed her name, his eyes dancing with mischief.

Calvin's heart leaped at the sight of the fine linen paper, such as someone like Bea might use. He repressed the desire to break the seal and instead tucked it inside his shirt. "Did you have a good meeting today?" A great deal of restraint kept him from asking about Bea by name.

"Not as many came today. I believe people hope the good weather of the last week will hold." Aunt Hilda gestured across the field where Tobias and Calvin had been working. "You have made good progress, I see. I continue to pray the Lord will reward your efforts come harvest time."

"What think you?" Tobias asked. "I might not be a farmer, but I've seen what hunger and cold can do to people. It seems wise to make plans in case the need arises."

"Beatrice suggested a plan at the last meeting. Something about gathering a portion of everybody's present stock and keeping it in a central place for emergencies. Kind of like what Joseph did in the Bible," Peggy said.

"Oh? Did she forward that plan again today?" Calvin hoped his ears didn't look as red as they felt.

Peggy and Aunt Hilda exchanged glances. "The Baileys didn't come to today's meeting."

"Too good for us," Aunt Hilda said.

"Ma," Peggy spoke reproachfully. She looked at her mother over her shoulder. "Mrs. Cabot said Mrs. Bailey sent her apologies, but unexpected business took them out of town."

"Out of town?" Calvin dredged the words out of his throat.

"I heard them say. . .New York," Peggy whispered.

Calvin's heart froze in place as hard as the earth after the last snowstorm. Once Bea arrived in New York, he might never see her again. Only the letter warming the space above his heart gave him any hope.

❧

"Mama. We have been to the dressmaker's shop three times

already, and we have yet another fitting scheduled. I already have far more than I need for our stay in Burlington." Beatrice looked at the storm clouds gathering to the north. *Please, heavenly Father, don't let a storm keep us from returning home as promised.* "And we've yet to go to the storekeeper in search of seeds."

"I thought Rose had given you some from her garden," her mother said.

"She keeps promising, but not yet. Besides, I want to see what varieties are available. I know what Aunt Rose has in her garden. The storekeeper may carry different stock."

Mama's harrumph told Beatrice she didn't believe it. "Tomorrow, dear, I promise we will do our best to go to the storekeeper. But today we must go to the milliner's to get hats to match your new garments."

Beatrice again looked at the gathering clouds. She suspected that come morning, Mama would use the excuse of the summer downpour to keep them from going out.

The time at the milliner's went more quickly than Beatrice had expected. She did enjoy a pretty frock, and seldom had opportunity to acquire fashionable head coverings such as the lace and muslin *coiffure à l'indisposition* that Mrs. Finch suggested, in a color to match her new outfit. Even more seldom did she have occasion to wear such finery, since she chose not to dress like a peacock when her friends' clothing resembled the equally beautiful but less colorful ducks and geese.

"I'll have the bonnets ready for you next Monday," Mrs. Finch said. Her own cabriolet bonnet, with the brim flaring away from her face, testified to her skill as a milliner and didn't look in the least out of place on her graying hair.

Beatrice tried to envision the same hat on Mama's head and couldn't. She wore clothes of the best quality, but no amount of the dressmaker's art could make her stylish.

"You seemed to enjoy your time in Mrs. Finch's shop," Mama said.

"Oh yes, she had a lovely assortment of hats. And illustrations of the latest fashions from Paris." Although when Beatrice would wear such things in Maple Notch remained open to question. "Will Papa bring them home?"

"Why, we'll pick them up ourselves. And you shall put on your favorite as soon as you step foot in the shop."

"But, Mama. . ." Beatrice hesitated before continuing. "We were supposed to stop in Burlington for no more than a week. It's been that and more already."

"Maple Notch will not disappear while we are gone" was Mama's only reply.

Beatrice looked at the storm clouds overhead and tugged her pelisse about her against the wind. Back at the house, she excused herself and went up to her chamber. Between Mama's less-than-forthcoming response and the gathering clouds that looked heavy with rain or even possibly snow yet again, Beatrice feared she might not make it back to Maple Notch any time soon. In fact, the new wardrobe, hairdresser, cobbler, and linens they had searched for all added up to one thing: New York. If snow fell, as she feared it might, Mama would seize on that as an excuse for not returning north.

Beatrice thought of the sums of money they had spent on clothing. The same amount of money could buy food and seed for the needy in Maple Notch. Why spend all that money on a summer frock that she might not wear this year if the weather remained cold, when others needed essentials?

She took out her reticule and counted up the money left from the sum Papa had given her to buy whatever "fripperies" interested her. The coins stung her hand, like money snatched from the mouths of children. She would spend no more. Papa had said she could spend it however she chose, and she knew exactly what she wanted to do. She had to get a letter back to Maple Notch.

She looked at the writing table waiting by the window. The cousin who used this room before her marriage was given to flights of poetry. She must have a supply of paper and ink nearby if it hadn't been removed since her wedding. Beatrice opened the drawer and found the supplies. Looking for a way to fix the dull pen nib, she dug in the corners of the drawer and found a knife to sharpen it. After a few exploratory scratches on the blotter pad, she began writing. She wanted to get her letters mailed before the weather closed in.

Beatrice addressed the first letter to Mrs. Cabot, explaining her desire to help with whatever plans the church ladies developed for aiding the poor, and enclosed her offering. She sprinkled sand to dry the ink while considering what to say in the second letter. Although Peggy would be interested in new styles, Beatrice didn't want to brag about her new clothes. She settled for saying, *"Mama has kept me busy dawn to night outfitting me with a new wardrobe. I fear she and Papa plan to take me direct to New York from here, without ever returning to Maple Notch. If their plan succeeds, I don't know when I shall return home again. Whether I shall come home again. You know their desire to see me married to a city man."* The ink from that last word spilled a little because of her shaking hands.

"Beatrice?" Mama said from the other side of the door.

"You've shut yourself up quite long enough. Your cousin has come to see you."

"I'll be there momentarily." Beatrice added another sentence to the letter before losing the will to do so. *"Storm clouds gather to the west even as I am writing. Please tell the farmers, and Calvin, that I am praying for the weather to remain warm. I am curious as to whether Calvin's experiment works out."* She scratched her name, addressed and sealed her missive, and tucked it into her bag as the door swung open.

"Beatrice! How lovely to see you again!" Her cousin Esther entered, face beaming with newlywed bliss.

Beatrice closed the flap of her satchel and settled down to enjoy her cousin's visit.

❧

An unnatural silence greeted Calvin when he awoke. The ordinary clucking of the hens and the lowing of the cows, usually audible in the cabin, sounded muffled. He knew even before he opened his eyes that snow had fallen during the night. Again. His stomach clenched. Today would be the true test of his radical idea.

Tobias scampered down the ladder from the loft, "Snowed again. Weirdest thing I've ever seen. It's as if we've moved to the northern provinces of Canada."

"Or that we're celebrating Christmas in July." Calvin forced himself out of bed to check on the damage. A brief glance out the window showed that snow dappled the new grass. "Could be worse."

Tobias leveled a look at him. "Could be better is what you mean."

Calvin shrugged and opened the door. The cold air that greeted him made him grateful he had kept his long johns on even in the height of summer. He took one look at his hearth and shook his head. Instead, he slipped on his outer clothes, coat, and boots and headed for the door.

"Hey! What about breakfast?" Tobias had started coffee.

"I'll be back." Calvin broke into a trot for the clearing.

Never had the sight of charcoal ash warmed his heart so. A few of the fires had gone out, but smoke still seeped from the majority of stumps. Best of all, no snow covered the growing corn mounds. The short green shoots stood untroubled by the night's storm.

"Hallelujah!" He jumped high enough to clear the pasture fence.

An echoing whoop sounded behind him. Tobias had shrugged on his coat and boots and followed him. The two friends threw their arms around each other and screamed. "We did it!" Calvin wanted to howl at the early morning sun. Instead, he ran up and down the rows of corn, checking to make sure he hadn't misjudged the state of the crop.

Tobias followed at a slower pace. "I'm no expert on farming matters, but these look about the same as they did yesterday. And that's good, right?"

"That's very good, my friend."

&

"Will you look at that." Uncle Stephen stood with his hands on his hips. "Your crops are growing right along as if this year has a summer after all."

"Warm the ground, keep the crops growing. Your cockamamie idea worked." Solomon crossed his arms over his chest. "You'll have half of Maple Notch by to see this marvel."

"Maple Notch? We'll have folks coming here from Burlington and beyond once they hear about it."

Burlington. One person who had prayed for his success wasn't here to enjoy it with him. Bea. Mr. Bailey had returned to Maple Notch in time to go to Sunday meeting last week, but the Bailey women remained absent. Peggy had ascertained they had indeed gone on to New York. Not even the missive he received from Bea could undo the worry settling around his heart.

"I fear it's too late in the growing season to start over again. Even if we could figure out how to duplicate trees roots since we've already cleared the stumps from our fields." Solomon bent down next to the nearest stump and cocked his head to one side, studying the rocks that held the chimney above the wood to vent it. "Looks almost like a smoke shack."

"Same principle. Slow and steady burn." Calvin allowed himself a moment of pride at succeeding where his older brother had failed. "I plan to share my crop with the family, of course."

Uncle Stephen clapped him on the back, but Solomon only grunted.

Tobias snapped his suspenders. "I keep telling him I'm his good luck charm, but he won't believe me for some reason."

"It's looking good." A new voice joined the congratulations. They all turned to study the newcomer. Hiram Bailey sat astride his horse. "I thought I would come see things for myself. And I must say it looks impressive, very impressive indeed."

Calvin could almost see dollar signs in the banker's eyes. For the first time, Calvin held the possibility of financial wealth and success in his hands—two things that might make him worthy of Hiram's daughter in the man's eyes.

So why did the calculating look in Bailey's eyes make his heart colder than the water flowing in the nearby stream?

six

Ice pellets smaller than chicken feed rattled the windows outside the bedroom where Beatrice was staying with her grandmother in New York City. Today she would not enjoy any of the diversions the city had to offer. No carriage rides, no paying calls, no afternoon salons. Not that it mattered. None of it mattered. The weather only reflected what she had felt inside since coming to the city where her parents had determined she should make her match.

Beatrice touched the window pane and traced a tree in the thin mist. She glanced around, fearful she might be caught in the act. Mama would scold her for creating more work for the servants, leaving fingerprints. Never mind; she would clean the glass later. She turned her head sideways and allowed her fancy to take flight. She drew some grass under the tree and beyond that, a simple rail fence. Something was missing. Her fingers moved without conscious thought to fill the void and created a row of mounds. A field, of corn and beans, the kind she had seen every summer in Maple Notch.

What nonsense. She wiped away the picture with her handkerchief and went for cleaning supplies.

Did the sleet here in New York mean snow fell, yet again, in Maple Notch? Beatrice prayed for the farmers, for the families whose lives depended on the yearly cycle of seedtime and harvest. This wasn't a famine as she had ever imagined it, yet the cold would create a shortage of food as surely as any drought.

She considered the half-eaten breakfast tray she had set outside her door with a guilty conscience. No one would suspect the scarcity of flour in Maple Notch if they spied the variety of pastries piled on her plate to tempt her appetite. As it was, she had lost so much weight Mama scolded her that they needed a dressmaker to alter her gowns. "You're getting too thin and pale. You must make an effort, dear."

She means well. New York, once the capital of the country, offered much to celebrate over the anniversary of American independence. The fireworks had surprised her, beautiful and terrifying at the same time. She had clapped her hands over her ears like a babe in arms. A number of young people laughed at her, behind their hands, of course. All except for one. Matthew Hubbard was presentable, a graduate of Harvard College, skilled with figures, from a well-to-do family—in a word, everything Papa wanted in a son-in-law. He also possessed everything most girls would want in a husband: charm, good looks, generosity—a man who loved God first and people second.

Only. . .he lived in the city. And even such a grand place as Grandma's house felt like a prison without the sight of the crops and smell of hay drying in the fields. She missed Maple Notch more than she thought possible. She wanted to know how the farmers were faring and if the ladies had succeeded in setting up a system for distribution to the needy; if Calvin's plan to keep his corn growing even during frost had succeeded.

Why not admit it? She missed Calvin. She took the cloth she had used to clean the window pane and dabbed at her damp eyes. Splashing cool water from the basin on her face, she gave in to the sobs that wouldn't leave her heart.

"Beatrice?" Grandmother Purcell's normally soft voice had an insistent tone.

Beatrice whirled around. "Grandmamma, I didn't hear you come in." She stood rooted to the spot, waiting for the scolding she was sure to come.

Instead, the agitated look on her grandmother's face disappeared, and she opened her arms. Beatrice took one step then stopped.

"Come here." Grandmamma nodded her head and Beatrice flew to her side.

Grandmamma led her to the bed, and they sat there together, Beatrice quietly sobbing while Grandmamma remained silent. When the muscles in Beatrice's back complained of their awkward posture, she realized how much time had passed. She lifted her head.

"There. We are quite alone." Grandmamma patted her hand. "Tell me what is troubling you."

Beatrice dabbed at her eyes with the still damp handkerchief. "I must look dreadful. What you must think of me, acting like a silly girl."

"Nonsense." That single word, spoken in her grandmother's sternest voice, brought a trembling smile to Beatrice's lips. "I have been looking forward to your visit for weeks, but you haven't been happy since you arrived."

"I didn't know it was so obvious." Beatrice blinked, her heart racing with renewed agitation. "I have done my best to please Mama and Papa."

"No one could ask for a better daughter. And you know your parents only want the best for you." Grandmamma stood and poured a glass of water before handing it to her. "But it seems God gave grandmothers extra eyes and ears. You aren't happy here in New York."

Beatrice feared tears would come into her eyes again, but she remained dry-eyed. She stood up and walked to the window, looking out at the sleet hitting the trees that swayed in the wind. "I wonder if it's snowing today back home."

"Surely not. Winter lingered extra long this year, 'tis true, but surely it won't snow in July, not even in Vermont."

"But it has. Every month this year. And the farmers are afraid they won't have a harvest this year if it snows again." She hugged her arms tight around her, as if to shut out the cold railing against the window panes. "And that is what troubles me. My friends and neighbors are facing a hard time, while I am in New York buying clothes and going to parties."

"Your father wishes to protect you from the harshness of life."

When Beatrice whipped around, Grandmamma raised a hand. "But he doesn't see that you are strong—strong enough for whatever challenges life might bring." She slipped a frail arm around her granddaughter's waist. "Remember this. No one's life is completely easy, whether they are in a palace or a log cabin. But I have faith you will persevere." She gestured to the tea tray sitting on the table. "Now will you eat a little to make your mother happy?"

Beatrice straightened her skirt and settled in the chair. The fragrance of hot tea teased her nostrils, and she discovered she was hungry. She poured herself a cup and noticed the bowl of strawberries, dewy and red as if they had just come from the fields. She groaned. "Strawberries. I love these, and ours hadn't come in." Her voice trailed off.

Grandmamma took a seat opposite her and leaned in close.

"I will speak with your mother. Perhaps between us, we can convince her to let you return home." She straightened and folded a napkin in her lap. "But until then, please at least pretend you enjoy seeing your old grandmother."

Grandmamma's rigid exterior had returned, but the twinkle in her eyes gave her away. Beatrice relaxed in the knowledge she had found an ally at last.

⁂

Calvin checked the fire on the last stump. The saltwater holes had long since burned away, but he decided not to create new ones. He didn't want to risk burning through the roots too quickly. He shook his head, wondering at himself. Ordinarily farmers begrudged the time needed to rid a field of a tree's root system, to free up more arable land. This year, Calvin wanted to slow down the process, keep the ground warm and pliable every day until winter set in again with full force.

"What's so funny?" Tobias asked. His face had by now taken on a healthy tan, and his shoulders had filled out. With what he had learned working with Calvin, he would make a good farmer if he decided to stay. He'd have his pick of the girls of Maple Notch—if he was looking. So far the only one he'd expressed any interest in was Peggy. Calvin grinned at that. Keep Tobias in the family. He liked the idea.

"I repeat. Why are you smiling?"

Calvin straightened the lines of his lips. He wouldn't tease Tobias about Peggy, not today, not ever. "I was thinking what a strange year this has turned out to be. Snow every month. Not even my grandparents have ever mentioned a year so severe, when they carry on about how bad things were in the old days, getting settled in the Notch."

"Then your smoking trees. Never heard of the likes of that

before." Tobias leaned on his hoe. "It's peaceful here. I see why you like it. Sometimes it's quiet enough that you can hear a leaf fall in the forest."

Calvin shook his head. "That's another strange thing. Usually I hear birds singing, at least in the mornings when I come out. This year it's been mostly quiet. I suspect the birds winged their way back south."

"The weather to blame for that, too?"

Calvin nodded. "A few succeeded in hatching a clutch. I'll show you a family of goslings I discovered the next time we go into town."

"Sunday morning. I can't wait."

He couldn't wait to see Peggy, but Calvin wouldn't mention that. He had his own reasons for wanting to see his cousin.

She had received word from Bea Bailey.

≥⋅

"Beatrice says she hopes to make it home by the end of August. Before, if she can convince her mother."

That was indeed good news after the string of descriptions of city life Peggy had relayed from Bea's letter as they walked to church Sunday morning. Tobias carried her basket while she relayed bits of news from the letter. Calvin strove to keep his face expressionless.

"There's no need to look as if you swallowed a lemon." Not enough to fool his cousin, apparently. "She *wants* to come back. That's a good thing, isn't it?" The three young people hung behind the others, talking together in low tones.

Calvin hesitated, but Tobias didn't. "Of course it is." He slapped Calvin on the back. "She'll be here in time to see how splendidly your crop is doing." His smile broke into a frown at Peggy's dour look. "I'm sorry. I know others aren't as fortunate."

"We'll get by. That's what Ma keeps saying. Pa says we might have to tighten our belts for a short time. Meanwhile when I go out to milk the cows, they look at me expecting their summer ration of grass in the meadow."

Tobias stuck his hands in his pockets, scowling, and Peggy seemed to realize she might have upset him. She glanced up at the sun and smiled. "But today is a lovely day and not a time to worry about tomorrow. This is the day the Lord has made. I will rejoice and be glad in it." She hummed a few bars of "Sometimes a Light Surprises."

Calvin put a finger to his lips. "Sh!"

"My singing isn't that bad, cousin." She grinned saucily and started singing again.

"Be still and listen for once."

Ears straining, they all waited. Calvin wondered if he had imagined it when there it came again. A soft *peep, peep.* "I told you we'd see them today!" He pointed in the direction of the river, across the brownish ground ordinarily high with green grass at this time of year. A line of fluffy yellow goslings waddled in a row behind their parents, whose brown feathers almost blended in with the background. "At least one family survived." *And so will we.*

The good weather and the sight of the goslings buoyed everyone's spirits. Even Parson Cabot seemed happy when he began his sermon. He preached from the eighth chapter of Genesis, when Noah and his family came out of the ark after the flood. "Last Sunday many of us struggled to make it to services because of yet another unseasonable freeze. This year has brought weather never before seen. I have heard some speculate that perhaps we are seeing the end of days, and the Lord must be coming soon. I am ready, but I do not expect it until I hear the trumpet call in the sky."

A few people in the congregation chuckled at that.

"But no matter how this year's weather has treated us, I want us to remember another time when the seasons were turned upside down. It rained for forty days and nights, so much water that all dry land was covered, even our beloved Green Mountains. After the flood, God gave Noah a promise. Does anyone remember the sign God gave Noah?"

A little girl with shiny black pigtails and wearing a blue pinafore answered, "The rainbow."

"That's right." The parson came out from behind the pulpit and bent over the little girl. "And tell me, what does the rainbow mean?"

"That there'll never be another flood." She scrunched up her face. "But it doesn't say anything about snow."

Laughter rippled among the adults, and the child's face turned bright pink.

"No, it doesn't." The preacher returned to the pulpit. "But I'll tell you what it does say. God promised that 'While the earth remaineth, seedtime and harvest, and cold and heat, and summer and winter, and day and night shall not cease.'"

As the words sank in, a hush fell over the congregation. Cabot waited before continuing. "I wanted to remind us of that. Seedtime and harvest will never cease. We may have a temporary aberration. But they will not cease. Harvest will come again. With a spirit of thanksgiving, let us raise our voices in the hymn 'The Sower.'"

The hymn was a favorite among the farmers, much as Jesus' parable delighted those who first heard it. From the first verse, "Ye sons of earth prepare the plough," to the last, "Father of mercies, we have need," the congregation sang with full voice, raising a joint prayer to the Lord, thanking Him for future harvests and trusting Him for the present.

After the service, no one hurried home. Instead, the ladies of the town had decided to enjoy a picnic under the sunny skies. Various colored quilts appeared on the ground. Even Peggy had packed one in the gigantic satchel Tobias had carried for her.

"Someone should have told us. We may be bachelors, but we could have brought something."

"Nonsense," Aunt Hilda said. "I'm sure the two of you will have your pick of dinners to share." She smiled at Tobias and Peggy, her cheeks dimpling in a rare show of good humor. "Including ours."

"Mr. Tuttle?"

Calvin allowed his gaze to wander while the speaker addressed his brother—*the* Mr. Tuttle in Maple Notch. No matter how many times he checked the gathering, he couldn't make the Baileys appear when they hadn't come to the service. Had Hiram indeed returned to New York? To fetch home his wife and daughter? He felt a smile creep to his face.

"Calvin, Miss Rusk is speaking to you," Aunt Hilda said.

"Mr. Tuttle—oh. I'm far too young to be Mr. Tuttle." The words stumbled out of Calvin's mouth before he could recall them. A look of chagrin passed over the face of the pale young woman standing before him, her arms holding a basket from which the savory smells of baked chicken arose.

"My mother said we could invite you to join us. As you see, we have plenty."

Calvin looked about for Tobias, but his friend had already taken a chicken leg from Peggy's basket. When another glance revealed no escape, Calvin gave in with good grace and walked with Frieda Rusk to the spot where her family was seated.

"Thank you for accepting our invitation." Mrs. Rusk's smile echoed and enlarged Frieda's shy look. "Frieda and I fixed enough food yesterday to feed half of Maple Notch. It's been too long since we had an excuse to celebrate summer."

Calvin nodded and bit into the stewed chicken. Taste melted into his mouth—far better than anything he or Tobias cooked up. He forced himself to chew and savor each mouthful.

Even after he slowed his pace, Frieda only managed one bite for every two or three of his. Her good cooking and generous spirit made up for her rather plain looks. She would make some farmer a good wife someday. *But not me.* He hoped she didn't interpret his presence on her family's picnic blanket the wrong way.

Frieda kept quiet, except to ask if he wanted a second helping of chicken or another corn cake. Her parents didn't bring much to the conversation either. The silence was broken only by occasional requests for more apple butter or squash. Across the green, Calvin saw Tobias and Peggy engaged in animated conversation and wished he were with them. He held back a sigh and tried to think of something, anything, to ask Frieda. His mind remained blank. After a second helping of everything, he demurred. "I can't eat any more and walk home. I'm so full, I'd slip on a stone and bust open. But it's delicious. Thank you."

She blushed. " 'Twasn't nothing."

Silence again descended while the others continued eating. When Mr. Rusk at last finished, he wiped his hand across his mouth. "I hear your crop is doing well. Your tree stump theory appears to have some merit."

"God has been good." Calvin hesitated to take credit. "We only lost a handful of plants with this last frost."

"Snow in July." The farmer shook his head. "Wouldn't have believed it if I hadn't seen it for myself."

"And your crop?" Calvin hated to ask but felt compelled.

"Gone." Rusk stood and gestured for Calvin to walk with him. When they had moved a few yards away, he said, "I don't like to say much in front of my wife, but our supply of seed corn is running low. If you have any extra next year, keep me in mind."

Seed corn. A thought danced around the edges of Calvin's consciousness but didn't take root. The success of his own crop remained in doubt, with the late planting. He didn't know if he would have seed corn available; and if he did, his family's needs would come first. But. . .

"I will keep that in mind, Mr. Rusk. But I still am not certain I will have more success than the rest of us."

Rusk's genial face turned serious. "I pray you do, Calvin. God help us if no one grows seed corn this year."

On the road home, Tobias and Peggy continued their lively conversation, while Calvin walked ahead of them, wrapped in silence. Was God giving him the opportunity to play Joseph to his Egypt, the people of Maple Notch? To provide food in a time of famine? *Right. If you're not careful, Calvin Tuttle, the next thing you know you'll imagine yourself the George Washington of Vermont. Or at least the Ethan Allen of the nineteenth century.* Try as he might to screen the possibility out, he couldn't stop thinking of options. If he had extra seed corn and sold it for a reasonable price. . .he could pay off the debt he owed the bank. He could make improvements to the property. *I could make a home ready for a wife.* Bea Bailey's face swam into his consciousness, but Calvin shook it off. *It will take more than the profit from one year's crop to satisfy her father.*

When he came to the wooden bridge that crossed the river to their farms, he paused. The others had lagged behind, and he was alone at the riverbank. Below him, water rushed by, still high from the constant runoff of snow this year. He wouldn't want to plunge into its icy depths. He took two tentative steps on its planks when a warning *snap* ripped through the air. Spreading from the center of the bridge in both directions, a crack appeared in two of the planks.

Behind him, he heard lighthearted laughter.

"Stay where you are!" Calvin called. He backed off the bridge with measured steps, almost running into Tobias.

"What did you say?" Tobias reached the bridge first.

Calvin flung his arm around his friend, pulling him back.

The other members of Calvin's family gathered around them. "What's the matter?" Solomon asked. "The wife is tired, and we're ready to get home."

Calvin nodded at the bridge. "Big crack. I fear it won't support any weight."

Uncle Stephen nodded and turned north. "Come, let's check out the larger bridge farther up the river." When Calvin didn't fall in with the family, he asked, "Are you coming?"

Calvin shook himself out of his trance. Weather, crops, Bea's letter, the bridge—it was too much to take in. Perhaps he should be glad circumstances disallowed him time to think about everything. He caught up with the others as they headed for the next closest river crossing.

Only a fool would cross the bridge with the danger so high.

seven

The cold drizzle couldn't dampen Beatrice's high spirits. Not when every *clip-clop* took her away from New York and closer to Maple Notch. Today they would reach the shores of Lake George. From there, they would travel by boat most of the way home. Along the way, they would pass Fort Ticonderoga, on Lake Champlain, which had played such a major role in the War for Independence.

Ticonderoga. As a child she had thrilled to the schoolmaster's description of the Green Mountain Boys' capture of the fort without a life lost. Unfortunately, when it fell during the second battle in 1777, two men of Maple Notch died: Solomon Tuttle and Donald Reid—Calvin's uncle and grandfather. Surprising that the same fort hadn't been a factor in the recent war with Britain.

Her grandfather had fought with the Green Mountain Boys, an experience they never discussed. But none of the men had died. What was it like for Calvin? Had his family told and retold their part in the struggle for America's independence? Is that what had inspired him to go off and fight when war broke out in 1812?

She shook her head to clear the thoughts of him in uniform—she had seen him once, with the tall shako felt hat and bright scarlet epaulettes—in the midst of a smoke-filled battlefield. She replaced that image with the way she had seen him last, sharing his idea for keeping the ground warm enough to grow a crop by smoking out the tree stumps. Thoughtful, committed, hardworking—these characteristics of the men that brought the republic into being lived on in their sons.

Overhead she heard a purple martin, the rich, gurgling call that awoke her on so many spring mornings. At least she thought it was a martin. She brought her hand to her forehead, blocking out the sunlight while she scanned the sky. Her thoughts went to the family of geese that had taken up residence on the town green after the goslings had hatched. The same geese returned summer after summer. Sometimes two or three pairs took care of as many as fifteen to twenty youngsters. This year, only one pair had remained on the green, with only four young. The cold weather had exacted payment from the local wildlife as well as the human population. Again she thought of Calvin and hoped his plan had worked.

She would see for herself soon enough; the road to Maple Notch took them past his farm. Her heart sped up, warming her skin as well as her heart, to the point she hardly noticed the cold air. How could she, when thoughts of the handsome young man who captured her heart's attention more than anyone else she had ever met filled her mind?

☙

"I know, it's cold and you want to get home." Calvin patted the neck of his gelding. "But I need to check on the bridge." With the horse's strong legs underneath him, he felt safe to go into the river. As he'd expected, the wooden planks showed signs of the year's bizarre weather patterns. Water had seeped into the wood, expanding in the damp, contracting when it heated and dried, increasing the crack. In a home, one patched spots if the damage grew too severe. But in a structure such as a bridge, a single crack could break a plank in half. Could they repair the damage or would they need to rebuild?

The crack had extended to within inches of the trestle. With his pocket knife, Calvin dug into the wood around the crack. Soft. Diseased. The crack might seal when the wood dried, or it might simply break apart. He'd discuss solutions with the family later.

He kneed his horse into movement, glad to leave the freezing water. The sky, sunny when he had arisen that morning, had clouded over and the air held a chill. *More snow?* He prayed it would be no worse than a cool rain and not another freeze. Could they have at least thirty days without a freeze before the next winter season snowed them in again? Would they experience summer at all, however fleeting?

With August fast approaching, he doubted it. Autumn began its inexorable descent into winter by the beginning of September. Summer's window of opportunity had almost passed them by. Only God's grace would allow him to grow any grain at all.

Horses whinnied and he looked up to see Uncle Stephen and his family on the road, accompanied by Tobias.

"We thought we'd come and take a look. Tobias told us where you were." Peggy glanced at him as she said it, a pretty pink blush staining her cheeks.

"What do you think?" Uncle Stephen asked.

"It's going to give way sometime soon, is my guess."

Aunt Hilda clicked her tongue. "That would be downright dangerous, with the river still so high."

And cold. But Calvin didn't say that. The womenfolk didn't need to know he had gone into the water. They would only rail at him for being so foolhardy. "I'm planning to block both ends of the bridge today, so people will know not to cross."

Uncle Stephen shook his head, a passing shaft of sunlight highlighting the gray streaks in his hair. "It will be a nuisance, to have to go north every time we go into town. Tomorrow I'll come back and make repairs. Easiest all around. Too much traffic passes this way to keep it closed for long."

Calvin hesitated but a moment. "I've been thinking of the traffic and the need for a safe crossing. We face this same problem every winter." He blew out his cheeks. "I'd like to build a covered bridge. And charge a toll to those who cross over it."

"A *toll* bridge? Why would we want to charge our neighbors?" Aunt Hilda sounded scandalized.

"A covered bridge?" Uncle Stephen puzzled.

"Someone in Pennsylvania came up with the idea a few years ago." Calvin looked at the bridge, envisioning the newer, stronger span that would replace it. "I crossed one when I was away to the war."

Tobias nodded his head. "I know the one you mean. Like a big old barn sitting atop a river. It felt rather spooky in there. An owl flew down from the rafters and hooted, and I near jumped out of my skin."

"Why would we want to do that? I helped build this bridge, remember. We've only needed to make minor repairs, at least until now. Leave well enough alone. We have other things that would do us more good, like a mill wheel." He added half under his breath, "If we get corn and wheat to grind."

Calvin bit back the protest on his tongue. So Uncle

Stephen didn't want to invest Reid family money in a bridge. And Calvin had precious little of his own. Not that it would take much. . .but he was already in debt to the bank, with repayment uncertain. Once again he sent his prayers heavenward for a healthy harvest.

"A covered bridge." Uncle Stephen shook his head. "Using tree roots to warm the ground and covering rivers with barns. What will you think of next, nephew?"

A lot of things. If only Calvin had the money to try them all.

&

Beatrice's heart urged the coach horses to plod faster, to eat up the miles remaining from the moment they had left Burlington and headed for the Notch, as some called it. But Papa was a cautious driver.

"Be careful now." Papa reflected her thoughts. "If you keep squirming, I'll wish we had stayed behind at the inn. After the ice last night, the roads are a little slick." Ice cracked underneath the horses' hooves, and water splashed on the sides of the coach as if to emphasize his point.

"Oh, Papa. It's a beautiful day." Sun glittered on the snow as it did after every storm, as if the world were once again created anew. "I even enjoy seeing snow again." She giggled. "I feel like I'm really and truly home."

At least Papa had allowed her to join him on the driver's seat. She twisted and turned, wishing she had a seat that could swivel and allow her to take in all directions at once. "Papa, you didn't tell me the trees had started to turn."

He scowled. "Did they ever grow leaves? We didn't even get our normal maple run this year. Business has been bad in every quarter."

Did he never think of anything besides business? "But look.

We are traveling on streets of gold and red and orange. It's as if we're headed for the New Jerusalem." She stretched out her right hand and grabbed a single maple leaf. "I feel like I can reach out and touch heaven from here."

Papa looked at her sideways. "You truly prefer the countryside to being in the city?"

How should she answer such a question? Papa seemed genuinely interested, so she tried. "When I'm in Maple Notch, I feel as though God is within reach in everything I see and touch. When I'm shut up in buildings crowded together and the only grass I can see is in the park, He feels more distant." She coughed. "I know God is everywhere, in the city as well as in the country. But it's just easier for me out here." She lifted her face to feel the sun. "In New York, I can't even see the sky properly for all the rooftops and carriages passing by."

Papa sighed. "I only want things to be easier for you. Life in Maple Notch is harsh. This year is proof of that. Any one of those young men your grandmother Purcell introduced you to could have given you anything you wanted."

After that, they both fell quiet, and Beatrice heard water rippling and crashing over rocks. "We're almost home!" Her voice rose in pitch. The falls lay to the south and west of the Tuttle and Reid farms. Soon they would reach the farms. Would she see Calvin this morning?

Through the trees, she caught sight of the water and heard the roar. By this time of year, she didn't expect to hear the water running so high or so fierce. Another sign of this year of no summer.

Then the road turned away from the river, skirting the edge of Solomon Tuttle's farm and making its way through the fields. The cleared land lay fallow, the only possible harvest hay to feed the animals over the winter. Had Calvin's crop suffered a similar fate? She caught her breath and urged the horse forward with silent pleas.

A short distance farther on, they crossed the boundary to Calvin's farm. A smoky fog hung over the fields, unlike the clear skies they had encountered elsewhere on the day's journey. Through the haze, she saw stalks of corn and poles of beans sprouting from the earth.

"Look, Papa!" Like a little child, she couldn't contain her excitement. "Mr. Tuttle's field is growing!"

Papa grunted. "He's done well."

Better than his brother's field. Maybe other farmers had succeeded in growing a crop. *Lord, let it be so. Our people need it.* She squinted her eyes, seeking a glimpse of figures working among the rows. Here and there the smoke stretched thin to reveal crops growing and prospering as they should. But Calvin and Tobias were absent from the fields. Her heart sank quicker than the sun behind the mountains. She didn't realize she had so looked forward to seeing him today. If not today, she wouldn't see him until Sunday at the earliest, with all of Maple Notch watching.

Papa clicked his tongue, and the horses picked up speed in the direction of the river. Had he slowed down to indulge her fantasy? *No.* Papa had allowed her to return home, but marriage to a farmer just starting out was still out of the question—at least in his mind. No, he was interested in Calvin's farm for reasons of his own. The young man probably owed money on the land—was Papa calculating the return on his investment? She opened her mouth to ask, then chewed on her lip. A direct question would only get an evasive answer.

"Leave business to the menfolk" or words to that effect. He had already given his comment on the state of the farm: well done.

As they drew close to the bridge leading on to Maple Notch, the sound of voices and ring of hammers filled the air. Papa checked the horses and slowed down as they approached. A gate stood across the bridge, barring their crossing, a man standing on either side—neither one of them Calvin. *Tobias,* and where Tobias was, Calvin was bound to be nearby. She looked and found him, waist deep in the roiling river water. She'd recognize that brown head of hair anywhere.

"We have company!" Tobias called out. He ran to the edge of the river bank and jumped over the barrier.

"Mr. Bailey!"

Calvin's head snapped up at the salutation. He caught sight of Beatrice looking at him; a lightning-fast glance passed between them before she looked away.

"And Miss Bailey. Thank the good Lord for your safe return."

"I should have made you travel in the coach." Papa spoke in a low voice to Beatrice. Raising his volume, he said, "Well met, friends! What has happened with the bridge?"

"The center planks cracked under the snow weight. Nothing we can't fix." Calvin's brother Solomon answered.

Calvin frowned a bit at that pronouncement. With his propensity for innovations, did he have something different in mind? She'd have to ask him the next time she caught him away from Papa. Maybe she'd misread his expression. She didn't want everyone to think she had been paying that close attention.

Papa was frowning. "At this time of year it's often possible to cross the river without the bridge." His statement of fact sounded like a challenge.

Mr. Reid came forward. "I wouldn't recommend that, sir. The water's high from so much snow melt this year. You want to protect your precious cargo." He smiled and bowed in Beatrice's direction. She felt heat burst into her cheeks and turned her face away.

"People count on this bridge to get into town. If they can't cross here, they have to go almost as far north as Franklin or down south of the falls. We need a reliable crossing to keep commerce flowing in and out of this neck of the woods."

"We're aware of that, sir. We should have the repairs completed and the bridge ready before the next Lord's Day." Solomon hesitated. "We are the ones most inconvenienced by the lack of a crossing. It cuts us off from town."

Would Maple Notch split into East and West, the way so many small communities did, all for lack of a bridge? Beatrice hoped not.

"I'll look for you on Sunday, then," Papa said.

Beatrice noticed the effort Papa took to control his features and smile at her. He thumped the top of the coach with his cane and Mama poked her head out the window. "We must turn back to the Southbridge crossing to reach home. We'll arrive later than we had hoped." Under his breath he mumbled, "I knew we should have stayed in Burlington."

❧

Beatrice was wondering if she would have an opportunity to speak with Calvin privately come Sunday, when she heard someone knocking at the front door. Her cat dashed to the door ahead of her, ready to greet their company. The parson's wife, Mrs. Cabot, stood on the doorstep.

"So glad to have you home. I was just informing your cook that the church ladies decided to hold a bake sale on Saturday. You know how they love to display their culinary skills," she said.

Preen their feathers. Beatrice didn't voice her thought. Instead she said, "We have many fine cooks in our community."

"Yes, we do." The smile Mrs. Cabot flashed at her let her know she guessed what she had been thinking. "And your cook has already committed to bring three pies. Now that you have returned, I wanted to clear it with you, and see if you wished to contribute something of your own."

Beatrice marveled at her skill in recruiting support. Mrs. Cabot could steal honey from a bear if she wanted to.

"And the purpose of the sale?" Mama had come up behind Beatrice.

"To raise money for the needy among us. So far, our income meets the demands, but we anticipate greater needs this winter." She coughed discreetly into her handkerchief. "Only a handful of farmers have succeeded in growing any kind of crop."

"Mr. Tuttle seems to have a fine crop." Beatrice feared she sounded boastful, but she had to express the admiration she felt at his accomplishment.

"True." Mrs. Cabot nodded. "Also, a few others have a number of plants that have survived the last two frosts that they hope will mature. But most have not. So—what would you like to contribute?"

Mama named a generous amount. Her parents had earned their reputation for contributing to worthy causes.

"I'll try my hand at making some lemon tarts," Beatrice offered.

Both women turned to look at her as if they had forgotten her presence. "But, Beatrice dear, Cook is already making pies. . . ."

"I'd like to do my part." Mama couldn't argue with that. That would give her an excuse to go with Cook to the sale. . . and see who came to bid and buy.

Mrs. Cabot beamed. "That is marvelous. I shall look forward to seeing you on Saturday. And perhaps you can remain after the auction to help us set up for school?"

School never started this early. "But it's only August."

Mrs. Cabot bent forward as if to impart a secret. "The school board thought it a good idea. The children aren't needed on the farms for harvest. In the spring, we can dismiss earlier so they can help with planting."

"Is my husband aware of this?" Mama's voice sounded high, the way it did when she struggled to keep a rein on her tongue.

"I'm not certain. The school board decided this past week."

Before Mama could interrupt again, Beatrice spoke. "We'll be happy to help. Does the school need any supplies?"

"Mr. Dixon has the list."

Beatrice made a mental note to check on a few families they often helped with what few school supplies were needed. A slate, chalk, some paper, and pencils. She thought of the books she had purchased while in New York. She would donate those as well, although perhaps she would read them first.

On Saturday morning Beatrice noticed people walking into town by midmorning, even though the bake sale wasn't scheduled to begin until eleven. The resident pair of geese honked to announce their arrival, chasing them away from their young—another thing she would miss in the city. She made herself stay in the kitchen, cleaning up from breakfast and shining the Franklin stove.

"That stove makes baking a lot easier than over the hearth, it does. No more scorchin' the puddings." Cook was kneading bread dough.

Beatrice nodded. "I never thought I'd finish the tarts so quickly. I should have volunteered twice as many." She laughed. "Or tried one of your recipes. I want to learn more."

"What for? You don't expect to fix the meals and turn me out of me home, do you?"

"I won't live in this house forever." *I hope.*

A smile chased around Cook's mouth. "Could that be why you're so anxious to get across the green?"

The geese honked again and dragged Beatrice's eyes to the window. She spotted Peggy. And where Peggy went. . .

"Go on with you. I'll get the maid to help me carry these things to the church."

"Thank you." Beatrice reached for the hat she had bought in Burlington. She was glad she had convinced the milliner to keep it simple. The plain lines of the empire dress and the mob cap matched and suited her coloring without looking out of place. Everyone said the pale rose color looked well on her. She hoped Calvin would agree. "Thank you for all your work. I know you didn't expect to be cooking our meals when you offered to bake for the sale."

"It's my pleasure. I'm only glad Mrs. Bailey didn't stop me when she came home." Cook downplayed her contribution, but her face beamed with pleasure. "Hurry on, now. Find us a good table to display our food."

Crossing the common, Beatrice lingered long enough to

enjoy the sight of children darting around the grass. A good number had turned out for the bake sale.

"Miss Bailey!" Young Amy Tuttle—Calvin's niece?—skipped to her side. "We heard you came back. Just in time for the fun! Will you join our team for tug of war?"

"I don't know." Beatrice looked down at her dress. Perfect for a tea party. Not quite designed for holding on to a rope with all her might and sliding through mud.

"Please join us." A deep voice added his plea to young Amy's. Beatrice turned around to find Calvin only a few feet behind her. "The Reids have challenged the Tuttles to a match, and Tobias has joined their side. The traitor." His eyes twinkled, and he nodded in the direction where his friend stood talking with Peggy.

"Is Peggy pulling?" Beatrice was curious.

"She's one of their best pullers. So you'll join us, then?" Calvin took her question as assent.

Beatrice gave one last thought to her new outfit. It could be repaired or even replaced if necessary. But a chance for a day of fresh air and friendship couldn't be repeated. "I will."

"Good. With you on our team, we're sure to win." Calvin's gaze held hers longer than was necessary or even prudent, and Beatrice turned in the direction of the tables. "Are the games before or after the sale?" She saw round loaves of bread made with fine-quality wheat flour, truly a delicacy. Spice cakes and dried apple pies and. . . She wanted to sample them all.

"We talked about that. Some were for having the games first, fearful people will gobble down the baked goods so quickly that they would get sick. Others said the games could get, uh, messy. Like the times we played rounders at school."

She giggled at that. The one time she had returned from school with her skirt muddied and her arm bruised from running the bases, Mama had been scandalized. What would she say if the same thing happened today, now that Beatrice was a grown woman?

"So we're having the sale first."

Beatrice fingered her reticule. She didn't have as much as she would like to spend. . .she always loved to buy and then help distribute food to those whose mouths had watered but didn't bid. But she had already sent a good part of her free money to Mrs. Cabot when she was in Burlington. "Do people have coin for a sale this year?" She asked.

Calvin shrugged. "That's not the only thing that's being bartered this year. Take a look." He pointed to a sign propped behind the table.

"That looks like the one from Dixon's store."

"It may be the same one."

Goods and services had been added as alternative forms of barter, with a cash value listed next to each. Everything from darning socks to bringing in hay had a price attached, as well as goods from spun wool to seed corn.

Calvin said, "People who don't have money to spend can offer their services, so everyone can take part. And your father has agreed to match every gift of services or goods with actual cash money, fifty cents on the dollar."

Beatrice sucked in her breath. What did Papa expect in return? Or was this an expression of unusual generosity?

"His offer has encouraged more people to join in. It pleased me when I heard of it."

Beatrice caught sight of Mama marching across the green as if summoned by Calvin's comments.

The look on his face told Beatrice her mother could undo all the goodwill her father's gift had engendered, at least in Calvin's mind.

eight

Calvin noticed Mrs. Bailey's approach at the same time Beatrice did. She probably wanted to steer her daughter away from her husband's biggest debtor. At least, it felt that way.

In spite of the thunderous look on Mrs. Bailey's face, she spoke civilly enough. "Beatrice, Cook needs your help in setting up the baked goods." She turned to Calvin. "I'm sure you understand."

"Of course." Calvin smiled politely while Beatrice moved in the direction of the tables.

Behind her mother's back, Beatrice glanced back at Calvin and mouthed *later*.

Without anything more to do until the bidding began, Calvin sought out Tobias. "What did Peggy bring?"

"Something with cranberries. It smelled heavenly." He tucked his hands into his pockets. "It's a good thing they have the barter system going. I doubt I have enough spare money to buy a single cookie."

Calvin chuckled. "I'm in the same predicament." The two of them had already discussed what services they could offer and how much time they could take away from the farm. If only Mr. Bailey would let him pay the debt on the farm with the same method. No, nothing but cold hard cash would satisfy the banker.

"What did Miss Bailey bring?" Tobias asked, a knowing gleam in his eye.

Calvin felt foolish. "I didn't ask."

"Then what were the two of you talking about? You carried on quite a long conversation."

Calvin laughed. "I invited her to join the Tuttle team in the tug of war."

"Do you think you're in the schoolyard? That's no way to a lady's heart."

A slender thread of memory tugged at Calvin's consciousness. "Lemon tarts. That's what she'll bring. That's what she always brought to school affairs. As I remember, they tasted wonderful."

"And what did that lady who fed you at the picnic used to bring?"

"Miss Rusk? I don't remember."

"Uh-huh." Tobias winked.

People gathered in front of the tables. The parson, who would act as auctioneer, stood behind the first table. "The ladies of Maple Notch have outdone themselves in preparing for this effort to raise money for the needs in our community. We've all felt winter's sting in this year of no summer. Remember that the bank will pay fifty cents on the dollar for every service offered in bid, so bid high and often."

Scattered laughter broke out across the crowd.

The bake sale wasn't like a box social; bidding involved no commitment between the parties beyond raising money for the community. Still, the transactions often told a tale of romantic interest. Even though the cook's name wasn't announced with the baked goods, one could usually guess.

A crock of Indian pudding came up for bid, and Calvin's brother Solomon called out, "A day in the hay meadows for anyone who needs help." No one bid against him, and he won.

Calvin scratched his head and walked over to join his brother. "Isn't that Hilda's pot?"

"Of course." Solomon looked surprised. "She's my wife."

Only a handful of people bid actual cash. Calvin hoped Beatrice's father wouldn't regret—or even rescind—his offer to match a percentage of the money raised.

Everyone enjoyed the festivities in a year that had offered few such occasions. Next up came a cream pie—Miss Rusk's specialty. Calvin clamped his mouth shut and tucked his hands around his sides, not wanting any miscommunication to the young lady who seemed to have set her cap for him.

Tobias had no such compunction. The plum pudding Peggy and Aunt Hilda had brought came up early, and he shouted out. "A day's general labor, whatever needs doing."

"You should only get half-credit for that day." Uncle Stephen teased the young man after he won the bid.

"I'll have you know I'm quite proficient at"—Tobias waited until he was certain everyone was listening—"burning out stumps."

People clapped, Uncle Stephen along with them.

Dishes came and went, but Calvin didn't see anything that tempted him to spend his money. No lemon tarts had made an appearance. At length the fine flour bread—baked by the Baileys' cook, he had no doubt—was offered. A few people bid cash for the quality bread.

Next Pastor Cabot, who served as the auctioneer, displayed lemon tarts. Calvin noticed they featured the fluted edge that Beatrice preferred.

He knew exactly what to bid for the privilege of buying every last tart.

ﾞﾞ

"Don't fidget," Mama whispered to Beatrice when her tarts were brought forward.

Beatrice didn't think she had fidgeted, not unless turning her reticule over in her lap once counted. Why had she offered to bake? She remembered the ignominy of one occasion when no one bid on her basket except her father. Barely sixteen at the time, she had felt the sting of that rejection for months. Only with time did she consider that her position as the banker's daughter might have influenced the outcome as well. She closed her eyes and prayed it would be different this time.

Mr. Reid gestured first. "We offer a skein of fine woolen yarn."

The man was so kind. Perhaps Peggy had suggested it.

"Two bits." Mr. Dixon's voice rang out. Had Papa asked him to bid on her offering?

"I said you had no need to worry," Mama reminded.

But they were all married men, not that it should matter.

"A bushel of seed corn after harvest. For all the tarts." Another voice offered, and silence fell.

Calvin.

The resident geese chose that moment to honk, and Beatrice's heart celebrated along with them. A bushel of seed corn was worth more than twice what anyone else had offered for anything. This year it would be worth its weight in gold. A gentle heat leaped into her cheeks. Calvin would do that. . .for her?

Parson Cabot's eyebrows went up at the bid, but he continued as if nothing unusual had occurred. "It so happens seed corn is what we need most of all. Does anyone have another bid?" After a beat, he said, "Lemon tarts, sold to Mr. Calvin Tuttle."

Beatrice could have melted to the ground on the spot, so warm her heart felt.

In contrast, the look on Mama's face could have frozen the hot tea waiting by the tables, but Beatrice refused to let her mother's dour mood dampen her spirits. "The seed corn will be much needed next year. What a wonderful gift." She didn't speak to the special feeling that ran rampant through her heart from a purchase that ran tantamount to declaring Calvin's interest in her.

The auction ended a short while later, although Beatrice paid scant attention. She had eyes only for Calvin, as he bit down on a lemon tart and offered a taste to Tobias. He refused, his own mouth probably full of Peggy's cranberry bread. Sounds buzzed around her, but she paid little mind.

"Come, Beatrice," Mama's voice intruded. "The auction has ended, and it's time for us to head home."

"I'm staying for the games." Beatrice smiled at her mother. "A summer frolic for the young people. I've been looking forward to this since I missed the last party at Grandmother's house." Mama couldn't refuse that request. They had worried that she didn't spend enough time with people her own age.

Mama pursed her lips as if to object, but what could she say? Get home before dark? That posed no problem, since dark lingered past the dinner hour, even in these waning days of summer. We have no one to bring you home? With home across the green, she'd remain within sight of the house at all times. Be careful of strangers? Her parents knew everyone in Maple Notch. In the end, Mama nodded. "I trust you know what you're doing, dear."

"I do." Beatrice bent forward and bussed her mother on the cheek. "I shall have fun and see you later."

Beatrice fought to restrain herself from skipping across the grass like a young child chasing a hoop and walked with the measured gait expected of a lady. Soon enough, she could appease her high spirits when the tug of war started.

On the near side of the green, the Whitsons and Frisks clustered around one rope. Beyond them she saw the Reids and Tuttles. Calvin motioned for her to join them.

"Good to have you on our team." He smiled at her. "You're the winning member."

"I don't know." Beatrice pretended to study the Reid family gathered on the other side. "Your uncle's mighty strong, not to mention Tobias."

"But then there's Peggy."

"What are you saying about me?" Peggy came close and offered a neck-to-ankle-length apron to Beatrice. "That frock is too lovely to endanger in the mud." She winked at her cousin. "And we *will* drag you through the mud."

Altogether, ten people grabbed either end of the rope. The harsh fibers felt rough on Beatrice's hands. She hoped she wouldn't make a fool of herself. "Take your place in front of me. I'll protect you." Calvin stood in front of Solomon, the two of them anchoring the rope, and she decided she would let the ropes burn through her skin before letting go.

Before they could exchange another word, the parson called, "Start," and Calvin pulled hard, the rope slipping through Beatrice's hands as if it was smeared with butter. Then it slid back as the Reids answered the opening tug, and she grabbed hold. What strength she had, she would add to the fight. She dug her heels into the dirt, pulled with all her weight on the rope, and yanked.

Yelling, grunting, even the rasp of the rope fibers on her hands faded as she fell into the rhythm of stumbling forward and yanking back. Ahead of her, Solomon's children pulled and hollered. Strain creased Peggy's face, and Beatrice imagined she looked much the same, facial muscles taut. Then the rope eased and slid through her fingers, and the release of pressure sent her tripping backward.

Into Calvin's arms.

❧

Calvin saw the dismay looming on Tobias's face before he felt the rope give way. He staggered and righted himself in time to receive Bea's falling body. His arms slipped around her waist and kept her upright. She felt so right, so natural there.

Without a thought to the people milling around the green or the congratulations flowing around them, he twirled Bea so he could see her face. He leaned forward, looking for permission in her brown eyes as deep and dark as gingerbread. Her lips, bitten to a cherry red during the effort to hold on to the rope, floated before him, inviting his caress. He brushed them with his own.

"Calvin." Solomon's voice intruded on Calvin's thoughts and he came to his senses.

He broke the kiss and tipped Bea's chin toward him. "I shouldn't have done that," he whispered.

"I wanted you to," she said.

"Mr. Tuttle!"

Mr. Bailey.

Calvin's face tingled with embarrassment. He tightened his palms into fists, then relaxed them before turning to greet the speaker. "Good day, Mr. Bailey." At least his voice sounded somewhat normal.

"You." The man shook with such fury that Calvin feared he might strike him. He took one step closer, but Calvin didn't budge.

"Papa." Bea put a hand on her father's arm.

"Go home and change your clothes. We will talk later."

"But, Papa—"

"Now."

She looked at Calvin, who nodded. *I'll be all right.* A frightened look he longed to erase still in her eyes, she did as her father asked.

If Mr. Bailey had noticed the unspoken conversation between the two, he gave no indication. "Come by my office on Monday morning. We have business to discuss." He turned on his heel as smartly as any military officer and walked away.

Calvin would have preferred an all-out fight to the unspoken menace.

❧

After no sleep on Saturday night, Calvin didn't fare much better on Sunday. He had been awake since before first light Monday morning. Sleepless hours had passed as he lay on his tick through the dark hours of night, waiting for the rooster's crow as an excuse to start morning chores.

Tobias joined him in the barn a few minutes later, rubbing his eyes, and sat down atop a bale of hay. "I didn't know you were ready to announce your interest in Miss Bailey."

"Neither did I." Calvin tugged too hard on the cow's teat, and she lowed her complaint in a loud voice. He considered himself lucky that she didn't kick him in the head and knock over the milk bucket in the process.

Neither one of them said any more. They had said it all before, on the way home Saturday and into that night, exploring the possibilities from every angle. Calvin had endured the censured gaze of everyone in the congregation at the Sunday worship service. Only one thing remained clear: Hiram Bailey held the title to Calvin's farm.

Calvin took the warm milk to the cool spring and drew water for the cabin. If he must confront Bea's father, he wanted to look his best. Tobias hovered by his side, silently supporting him as he had all during the war. When at last Calvin left the farm, Tobias said, "My prayers go with you."

"Thanks. I need them." Calvin didn't know that even a prayer meeting with every member of his extended family in attendance would sway Hiram Bailey's mind. Only a genuine God-given miracle would save him from the wrath of the banker.

With the crack in the bridge repaired, Calvin made good time, planning to reach the bank before it opened. Every minute since Bailey's summons had lasted as long as a century. He wouldn't postpone the meeting any longer than necessary.

The air held a chill bite on this late August morning, and Calvin feared snow might fall yet again. He looked in the direction of the Bailey house on the opposite side of the green. This morning he yearned for some twitch of a curtain or other sign that Bea was watching and waiting with him. That way lay heartbreak, he knew. She might not even know about her father's demand, since she had left before he issued his challenge.

But Bea said she wanted to kiss me. Calvin tucked that memory into his heart. Determination to declare his intention surged through him. He straightened his shoulders and strode with firm steps to the bank, turning the handle. It didn't budge. Closed. He was debating what to do next when he spotted Paul Cabot, the parson's oldest son and the bank clerk, heading in his direction.

"Good morning, Mr. Tuttle." The young man had a good head for numbers and an inoffensive manner. "Mr. Bailey told me to expect you this morning." He turned the key in the lock and let them both into the dark recesses of the building.

Calvin had entered the bank only once before, when he finalized the loan for his land. Then as now, the cool shadows alternating with bars of sunlight from the windows attracted his attention. As striped as a jail cell, and as secure, only the items under lock and key were hidden in a vault built into the back wall. He'd heard that Mrs. Bailey kept her silver set in the bank except for special occasions. Imagine having something that you'd need to lock up for safekeeping. Almost everything he owned had been made at home and could be replaced with time and effort.

How could someone like Bea, used to fine silver and fancy dresses, ever be interested in him? But she said she was.

Young Cabot lit a fire in a small grate and placed a tea-kettle over it to boil. "Mr. Bailey likes his tea when he arrives."

Calvin wondered how long he would need to wait. To think he had expected the banker to be at work shortly after sunrise. Restless, Calvin wanted to pace back and forth. The bank building wasn't much larger than his own house; but aside from the counting desk, teller window, and a small partition for Mr. Bailey's office, the space was empty. Calvin made himself stay in the chair and kept his feet on the floor. He wouldn't betray his nervousness, not even to the clerk.

Cabot had time to open the cash drawer behind the counter and prepare the tea before Mr. Bailey arrived.

"Mr. Tuttle. You are here already. Good. Come this way."

"Shall I bring tea in, sir?" Cabot asked.

"Later." Bailey waved him away.

So this wasn't a social occasion, but Calvin already knew that. He followed Bailey into his office.

The man sat in his chair and steepled his fingers without speaking. He turned so that Calvin could see only his face in profile, and the likeness to Bea startled him, although her face was softer, rounder. They were father and daughter, after all, but. . . The silence lengthened and tested Calvin's resolve. He decided to make the first move.

"Mr. Bailey, you must know I hold Miss Beatrice in the highest regard."

Bailey swiveled his head in Calvin's direction. "Is that why you dragged her through the mud—literally—and kissed her for all to see like a common hussy?"

Heat invaded Calvin's cheeks, but he kept his voice even. "I regret the circumstances, sir, but I will not deny the feelings I have for Miss Bailey. I would consider it an honor if I had your permission to court her." There, he had said it. All the breath rushed out of his chest, and he couldn't have spoken again if a knife was held at his throat.

Bailey's eyebrows rose, and he studied Calvin with the brown eyes so like Bea's. Had the man considered forcing a wedding between the two? Some might feel it appropriate, even necessary, after the way they had embraced yesterday. The banker gave no clue to his feelings as he rose to his feet. At the window, he looked south, in the direction of the more settled communities in their new country. "I had hoped for better things for my daughter than to be stuck in the countryside. But she chose to return to Maple Notch."

So Bea had forced the return to Maple Notch. Some of the icicles of fear around Calvin's heart melted.

Bailey returned to his chair and looked Calvin straight in the eye. "But even here, I will not allow my daughter to marry any ordinary man who catches her attention. That includes you, Mr. Tuttle. You do not even own your own property free and clear."

Once again, Bailey steepled his fingers and tapped them together. "You are a man with innovative ideas. You alone have succeeded in protecting your entire crop for harvest. And I have heard rumors that you are considering a toll bridge, one covered overhead like a barn."

Calvin cleared his throat.

Bailey pointed his index finger at him. "Listen to me. I for one wish to see industry and innovation rewarded. When your harvest comes in, I would like to buy the bulk of your seed corn for five dollars a bushel. That kind of money will satisfy the lien on your property as well as provide some extra. A man with that kind of security might be worthy of my daughter." He leaned forward, brown eyes boring into Calvin. "What say you, Mr. Tuttle?"

nine

Five dollars a bushel. The words exploded inside Calvin's brain as he made his way home. No one ever paid that kind of money for seed corn.

No one ever needed to. Most years, corn was abundant. Often more grew than people could use for food or seed, and the extra went to fattening hogs.

Five dollars a bushel. The words kept repeating themselves in Calvin's mind, taunting him, tempting him.

The lien on his property, satisfied like that, with a snap of his fingers. More money available for other improvements. Calvin reached the bridge, repaired and sound enough for another winter, and thought about his desire to build a covered bridge. The money the banker offered would provide for that project, which would in turn bring in additional income in the future.

"A man with that kind of security might be worthy of my daughter." The words trotted through Calvin's heart as his feet plodded ahead.

Is this Your answer, Lord? Calvin threw the question to heaven, but he received no answer, not even a snowflake, in reply.

Tobias was hard at work in the field when Calvin rode in. Why did he feel so reluctant to share the good news with his friend? His success also meant success for Tobias. What was holding him back?

Tobias didn't wait but instead raced across the field to meet Calvin. "I expected you back some time ago. Tell me. Did he demand payment? What are you going to do?"

The quick questions reminded Calvin of their shared concerns and the prayers they had offered together during the night. He shook his head. "Not exactly." He drew a deep breath. "In fact, *he* offered to pay *me*."

"What?" Tobias jerked upright.

"He wants to buy my seed corn."

"For some ridiculous price, I suppose? Take advantage of you?"

"Actually, no." Calvin heard the surprise in his voice. "He offered me five dollars a bushel."

Tobias whistled. "Even I know that's a lot."

Calvin's smile soured his stomach.

"What's wrong? That's good news, isn't it?"

"Better than demanding payment in full in cash." Calvin began the slow walk across the clearing. "You and I both know he's not doing it out of the goodness of his heart. He wants to make money."

"And—?"

"And that means he'll resell the corn to my friends and neighbors. Maybe even my family. For even more money, more than they can afford."

"Oh." Tobias slid down to the ground.

Calvin grabbed his hoe and began scratching at the ground. He didn't feel like working, but eating and talking appealed to him even less. Maybe physical labor would provide the clarity he needed.

❧

Contrary to Papa's threatening tone at the bake sale festivities, he hadn't done more than confine Beatrice to the house since Saturday. In other years, she might have chafed at being kept inside, away from her garden. But after the recurring freezes, she had given up hope for anything more than a potato or two. She wished she had tree stumps to smoke out.

Like Calvin. She looked out the window again. She had heard Papa's demand to meet with him this morning as she walked back to the house. What had transpired between her father and young Mr. Tuttle? Had Papa taken the anger that rightly fell on her shoulders out on Calvin? She swallowed past the lump in her throat. Patches, her cat, jumped onto her lap and pushed her head against Beatrice's hand.

A light knock sounded on her door.

"Come in."

Bessie, her maid, bringing the rose dress Beatrice had worn to the bake sale with her. She hung the dress in the armoire and stood back to study it. "It turned out right nicely, Miss Beatrice." Not a word of complaint for the additional work Beatrice had created in soiling the nearly new dress, only pride in a job well done.

"Thank you, Bessie. I'm sorry to have created so much additional work for you."

The maid started to leave, but Beatrice stopped her. In a fit of remorse, she went to her armoire and hunted for the lilac sprig frock that had pleased her so. It would look good on Bessie, with her coloring. "Take this. I shan't need it any more."

"But Mrs. Bailey. . ."

"Mama won't object. I'll explain."

After profuse expressions of gratitude, Bessie left. Beatrice sighed. Soon she must join Mama in the parlor, where another sewing lesson awaited her.

If only she could find a way to get rid of the ugly feelings inside, even as laundry was pounded against a rock, scrubbed, and ironed. Not that Beatrice had actually ever washed clothes—a skill she would have to acquire if she married anyone from Maple Notch. She didn't know how to be a proper farmer's wife. Perhaps she should marry one of the city men Papa had taken such pains to introduce her to. At least then she'd know what was required of her.

Stop thinking like that. She lifted her chin in the air. "I can learn." She spoke aloud to reassure herself. "I'll make my own clothes instead of stitching samplers. I can even learn how to spin and weave if I have to."

"What's that, dear?"

Beatrice twirled around. "I didn't know you were there, Mama."

Her mother came into the room, set down a tea tray, and fingered the dress Bessie had cleaned. "It turned out well." Like Papa, Mama hadn't spoken of the scene at the bake sale, as if their silence could make the memory disappear. Their kindness felt undeserved.

Remorse for disappointing her parents sent a pang through Beatrice. "I was preparing to come downstairs."

"Sit down, dear." Mama took one of the chairs by the window. "There's something your father wants me to talk with you about."

Uh-oh. Here it comes. Beatrice relaxed the fingers that had clenched her dress and set down across from her mother, folding her hands in her lap. Avoiding looking at her mother, Beatrice gazed out the window. How could the sun shine so brightly when a chill had settled over her heart?

Mama didn't speak for a minute, instead busying herself with the niceties of pouring tea and stirring in a bit of cream. Memories of the childhood ritual lingered, occasions when Beatrice felt her heart would break and Mama offered comfort. Encouraged by the sign, Beatrice relaxed.

"Eat a bite of the shortbread, dear. We are concerned that you have lost weight recently."

Beatrice obediently bit into one of Cook's flaky delicacies, even though it tasted like ash in her mouth. She managed to eat two of the cookies, drinking two cups of tea. Mama was right. She *did* feel a little better after consuming some food.

Mama peered at her, as if assessing her state of mind. Apparently satisfied, she took her tea cup in her hand and held it to her lips, her little finger extended. "Your father has always hoped for you to have an easier life than we have here in Maple Notch. But when I told him of your obvious distress in New York. . ."

A sad smile flitted across Mama's face, and she set down her cup, staring resolutely at Beatrice. "Mr. Bailey met with Mr. Tuttle this morning."

Beatrice's heart tripped. "What happened at the sale. . . It wasn't his fault. It was mine. I shouldn't have agreed to the tug of war."

"That's as may be." Mama's gaze flicked to the repaired dress hanging in the armoire. "Mr. Tuttle might as well have written a message in the stars to do what he did. Everyone in Maple Notch will expect the two of you to begin courting seriously, perhaps even to read the banns."

Beatrice's heart skipped. Did her liking for Calvin extend to love? Was she ready to. . .marry? She thought she knew the answer. Heat flooded her cheeks and ran along her limbs to her fingers, where she touched the cup of hot tea.

"I would not speak so plainly if not for the outrageous behavior of the two of you. We felt we must act quickly. Mr. Bailey has come up with a plan that will ensure Mr. Tuttle's future without harming his pride."

When Mama didn't continue, Beatrice ventured a question. "What does he have in mind?"

A secret smile played around Mama's lips, satisfied that she had hooked her daughter's interest. "Mr. Bailey had already taken note of Mr. Tuttle's innovations. He would have offered him assistance sooner or later, only perhaps not so quickly."

Tell me.

"Your father is prepared to buy Mr. Tuttle's seed corn for a healthy amount. Providing he is able to harvest it, which it appears he will. One of the very few this year, as you know."

Pride flowed through Beatrice's heart. Calvin had succeeded. "But what will Papa do with corn?" Beatrice puzzled. He was a banker, not a merchant.

Mama shrugged. "Does it matter? After this year's poor harvest, he feels it is a wise investment. In return, he promises that Mr. Tuttle is welcome to court you once he satisfies the lien on his property." Mama's smile was genuine this time, a lip-stretching, teeth-showing grin. "You see, your father only wants to make you happy, after all."

A crumb of Cook's shortbread remained on Beatrice's plate, and its buttery richness appealed to her palate. She took another cookie and bit into it, savoring taste for the first time in several days. The sky looked bluer, and even the struggling grass managed to look green.

The world was made anew—for her and Calvin.

❧

The remainder of the week passed in agonizing slowness for Beatrice. She felt every second—eating enough to please even Cook, preparing seed to feed birds during the coming winter, watching the world outside her window. During her sewing sessions with her mother, she worked on a wedding gift for Peggy. The entire town expected an announcement at any moment.

In spite of all the activity, or perhaps because of it, the hours stretched from daylight to nightfall. She couldn't wait for Sunday, when she would have an opportunity to see Calvin.

"Am I allowed to speak with Calvin, then?" Beatrice asked during conversation with her mother.

Mama clucked. "It isn't seemly for you to chase him. Let him seek you out."

Monday went by. . . Tuesday. . . Wednesday. She'd hoped to receive word of some kind from Calvin, certain he would rejoice with her. Had he repented of the kiss they had exchanged after the tug of war? That thought sent a cold stab of fear through her heart.

Or maybe he's working all the harder on his farm. Now that Papa had agreed to their courtship in principle, perhaps Calvin had thrown himself into producing as much seed corn as possible. That thought offered a little reassurance.

Perhaps Calvin wouldn't speak with her until he had met Papa's conditions, once he had sold the corn and paid the bank. Never had the weeks until harvest stretched so far into the future.

On Thursday a light snow fell. Although not an unusual occurrence for early September, it signaled the beginning of the traditional snow season. To her relief, Indian summer returned the following day.

She decided to take advantage of the pleasant weather and approached her mother at breakfast. "I plan to go out today. To the store and to the parsonage."

Mama's eyebrows knit together then relaxed. "Be certain you wear your coat. The air may still hold a chill after yesterday's snow, and I hear some have taken sick."

"Of course." As long as Mama agreed to her going around the green unescorted, Beatrice would agree to anything, even wearing mourning. After so many days housebound, she longed to get outside and perhaps meet someone her own age. "Mr. Dixon expected new books in his next shipment." Hoping to forestall the complaint she saw forming on Mama's tongue, Beatrice hastened to add, "I also want to look at woolens. I'm thinking of making a cape for Papa for the winter."

Mama put a finger to her lips. "I won't say a word. Do you need Bessie to accompany you to help carry your purchases home?"

"No. If there is too much, I will arrange for Mr. Dixon to deliver it." While Beatrice enjoyed Bessie's company, she hoped for a few minutes of privacy. "If I meet a friend at the storekeeper, may I invite her home?"

"Of course." Mama smiled as if she had known Beatrice's true plans all along. "Today is market day, isn't it? I shall tell Cook to expect company for tea."

After a few minutes to gather her market basket, tie a bonnet under her chin, and don her cape, Beatrice headed out the door. Trading her slippers for boots proved a wise choice in light of the muck underfoot, still muddy after yesterday's snow. The green seemed barren without the family of geese.

Since the young had matured, they'd disappeared the day before the snowfall, heading south to whatever warmer climes best suited their needs. She heard honking overhead and looked at a small group, perhaps only a single family, flying in the familiar V formation. Few flocks swarmed overhead this fall, translating into fewer geese to shoot and dress for hungry families.

Away from the shadow of the house and trees, the air felt remarkably warm, as pretty as a spring day, without the nuisance of the bugs that thrived in the early season. Unbuttoning all but the top button of her coat, Beatrice allowed the breeze to lift her skirts in a dance that matched her high spirits. She found a single red leaf by the side of the road and stopped to pick it up. With care, it might remain whole until she reached the house, where she could press it between the heavy volumes in their library. Dried leaves provided much opportunity for creativity during the winter months. She studied the ground for further material for floral arrangements. In her joy at being out of the house, she temporarily forgot her destination.

"Beatrice? Is that you?"

At the sound of Peggy's cheery voice, Beatrice looked in the direction of the river road. Calvin and Tobias accompanied Peggy. Not wanting to appear overeager, Beatrice retrieved a couple of pine cones before she straightened to her full height and walked toward them.

"Good afternoon, Mr. Heath, Mr. Tuttle." She was certain her face must be as red as a holly berry, but no one seemed to notice. Calvin appeared as discomfited as she felt, but she maintained her pretended indifference as she reached the trio.

Only Tobias seemed unaffected by the mood. "It's days like

this that make fall my favorite season of the year." He peeked into her basket. "And you are gathering leaves."

"I use them to make floral arrangements during the winter months." Beatrice paused. How trivial that must sound.

"Yes. She makes marvelous things, doesn't she, Calvin?" Peggy's eyes danced with mischief. "We always save our corn silk and a few ears of Indian corn for her to use."

Calvin nodded in reply. So far he hadn't spoken. He had never seemed so reticent in her presence.

"Come, Mr. Heath," Peggy said. "It's time we played that game of checkers you promised me."

"I did?" Tobias took a second look at Calvin and Beatrice. "Oh, yes, *that* game. Well, Calvin, you know where to find me." He tucked Peggy's arm into his elbow and walked to the store, her soft giggle trailing behind them.

"That was a tad heavy-handed." Beatrice felt compelled to speak when Calvin still did not speak.

At last, Calvin relaxed and chuckled. "Come, let's not waste this opportunity they've provided us. We need to talk, you and I." He reached out his hand an inch before sticking it back in his pocket. "I would offer you my arm, but I'm afraid tongues will wag more than they already have—even if we are in full view of everyone in town today."

Beatrice relaxed enough to giggle herself. "We shall walk around the common with a foot of space between us, then." They strolled at a pace more appropriate to baby's toddling steps than to adults. The point wasn't to arrive at a destination, but the time they spent together.

Beatrice waited eagerly to hear what Calvin had to say.

❧

Calvin couldn't bring himself to meet Bea's eyes. Those dark brown pools invited him to jump in and bask in their warmth. They reached the spot where they had won the tug of war, and he had taken advantage of the situation by kissing her. Resolutely, he stopped walking and turned toward her.

"I was wrong to take advantage of you at the bake sale. I have no excuse, except that you were in my arms, and. . ."

"And it seemed the most natural thing in the world. I know."

Her soft answer took Calvin by surprise. "You're not. . . offended?" He allowed himself to look at her.

This time, she was the one who dropped her eyes. A becoming pink colored her cheeks. "No."

That one word gave Calvin the courage he needed to speak further. "Your father spoke with me on Monday morning."

"Yes, I know." Further pink slammed into Bea's cheeks. "I noticed you walking into the bank."

"So that twitch of the curtain wasn't just my imagination?" Calvin allowed a teasing note to enter his voice.

"I was afraid of what Papa would do."

Concern raced through Calvin. "Was he harsh with you?"

"No." An unreadable expression crossed Bea's face. She bent to pick up a leaf. "Is it forward of me to ask what you discussed?" She bit her bottom lip, as if afraid of his answer.

Had Mr. Bailey said anything to his daughter? Did she know her father had opened the door wide for him to call on her? His mouth went dry. *Lord, help her understand.*

"He asked me about my crop, if I expected to have extra seed corn. I suppose he had heard my bid for those lemon tarts at the bake sale."

A smile played around Bea's mouth. *Good.* "Did you enjoy them?"

"They were as good as I remembered from school. I expect anything you make would be delicious." He smiled at her then, and she returned his smile. He could have drowned in the happiness he saw reflected in her eyes. He sighed. He had to tell her. "I told him, yes, I expected to have more corn than I can use myself. And so he offered to buy it."

He studied her face, looking for signs of surprise, and saw none. *She knows.* Was it even her idea? No. Mr. Bailey wouldn't make business decisions based on his daughter's recommendation.

She lowered her lashes. "What did you think of his offer?" Her voice sounded small but hopeful, as full of promise as one of the acorns she bent over to pick up from the ground.

"It was a very generous offer." That was true.

"So you'll accept?" Hope lit her face like a candle burning in a window on a dark night.

Lord, help me find a way to say the next, hard part. He glanced around the common, seeking a way to avoid the topic for a while longer. The church beckoned, but they couldn't go there as long as they were alone. The entrance to the emporium yawned open on this beautiful Indian summer day, but he didn't want to announce their business to the world.

No, this spot on the Maple Notch common would have to serve as the place where he opened his heart—and left himself vulnerable to her misunderstanding and rejection.

"I can't. I'm sorry, Bea, but I can't."

ten

Beatrice felt her mouth open in a silent scream. He *couldn't* accept Papa's offer? She backed away. "No, I'm the one who's sorry. I must have misunderstood. . . ." She turned in the direction of the store and took two hurried steps.

"Bea, wait."

How dare he use that nickname when he'd just broken her heart?

Calvin's hand landed on her arm, gentle and soft, not harsh like the pronouncement he'd made.

"It's not for the reason you think." His face had paled and hardened. The same expression she had seen on men's faces when they talked about being in the war. "I would do almost anything to win your hand." The words blurted out of his mouth, and he looked surprised that he had said them.

Heat crept up her neck and ears and into her face. She didn't know whether to feel angry or happy. "Almost anything?"

"Did you ask yourself what your father would do with all that corn? He doesn't need it. He's not a farmer."

"I suppose he would sell it. What does it matter? You'll have your money."

Calvin hung his head, staring at his boots, before he straightened his back and looked at her. "Come with me." He led her to the corner where they could see the paths leading out of town. "Over that way the Whitsons live." He pointed to the east. "And farther south on this side of the river, you'll come to the Frisks' farm." He went on to mention several families who lived in their community. "Who do you think will buy the corn?"

"Anyone who needs it. Mr. Dixon might act as the broker. What's the problem? Don't you want your neighbors to have your corn?" His obvious discomfort didn't make sense to her.

"He'll want to sell it for more money than he paid me."

"Of course." Beatrice nodded.

"But don't you see?" He sighed and moved his hands through the air like a teacher explaining something to a difficult pupil. "They won't be able to afford the prices he'll have to charge. They'll borrow money from his bank. It will be like what happened in Egypt during the famine. First the people sold their crops to Pharaoh, then their land, finally themselves. And I won't do that to my friends, neighbors. . .my own family. Putting everything people have made for themselves here in Maple Notch at risk." His gesture encompassed all the surrounding farms. "Not so I can make a small fortune." She saw tears in his eyes. "Even if it means losing my chance with you."

All breath drained from her body, and she willed herself to remain upright. She felt as though she had been led to a mountaintop, where she could gaze over all the wonders of the world—and then been pushed off.

"You're wrong." She forced the words through clenched teeth. "You *can* accept Papa's offer." She put up her hand when he started to object. "But you won't." She blinked back the tears that threatened to pour out of her eyes. "Maybe you are just a poor farmer with no more sense than God gave a rabbit, like Papa always thought." She grabbed her basket close to her chest and walked with quick, determined steps in the direction of her house. Her senses searched for some sound, some sign that Calvin had followed her.

All she heard was the wind whistling through the empty tree branches.

ᴥ

The next day, Papa called Beatrice into his study before supper. She took a moment to compose her features before she entered. Even then, she stood at the door rather than sitting down in the Windsor chair.

"Sit down." The way he almost barked the request made her heart quake. Her legs shook as she settled into the chair and clutched the armrests.

Papa frowned at something going on behind them, perhaps Bessie cleaning in the hallway. After he closed the door, he took the seat next to Beatrice's instead of behind the desk. He took her hands in his, his dark eyes harboring a degree of kindness she rarely saw there. "Calvin Tuttle came to see me today."

Speechless, she swallowed, not sure if she wanted to hear what was coming.

"He refused my offer." Papa's voice sank deeper with every word, trailing off at the end. He studied their clasped hands as if searching for a reason why a man would do such a thing. When at last he raised his eyes to meet hers, she saw pain etched in lines around their corners.

But his mouth was set in familiar, angry lines. When he spoke again, his words came out clipped and hard. "He told me he discussed his reasons with you. I told him that any man with no more concern for his future than that had no business courting my daughter. He still refused my offer."

Beatrice flinched at the hot anger radiating from her father. Her own angry hurt rose in her throat.

"I did the best I could for you, my dear. You asked to return home. You expressed interest in this farmer—in a most brazen way. He has turned his back on both of us. Unless we suddenly discover a diamond in the rough among the other young lads of Maple Notch—something I sincerely doubt—you *will* return to New York. Your grandmother will see you properly wed."

"Yes, Papa." Beatrice held back her sobs until she reached the sanctuary of her room, where her tears scalded her cheeks at the thought of her father's heavy words.

❦

Tobias put a hand on Calvin's shoulder as they approached the meetinghouse on Sunday. The Bailey family arrived at the same time, the two parents flanking Bea like prison guards. Even with his heavy heart, Calvin couldn't help noticing her glorious appearance. Golden ringlets framed her sweet face and drew attention to her doe-brown eyes. In spite of their painful parting, his heart still raced to meet her even while his feet slowed.

He knew the moment Bea saw him. Her chin came up, and she turned her face away. She had spurned him as thoroughly as though she had shouted aloud.

Calvin stopped moving, then forced himself to walk forward. *Pretend nothing is wrong.*

"I'll find a way to talk with her today, Calvin. She has no right to treat you this way," Peggy said, her face flushed from Tobias's gentle teasing.

Calvin shook his head. "Her father's even more set against me than he was before, and no one makes an enemy of Hiram

Bailey without cost. And if Bea"—he swallowed past the break that his voice wanted to make—"if she agrees with him, then she's not the woman I thought she was." Once again his pace quickened, and he intercepted the family on the threshold of the meetinghouse.

"Good day, Mr. Bailey. Mrs. Bailey. Bea." Calvin greeted them as if they were no more than casual acquaintances. "This is the day the Lord hath made." He smiled, indicating all was well and inviting them to finish the verse.

Sparks flashed in Mr. Bailey's eyes. Bea's eyes focused on the ground. Only Mrs. Bailey showed any degree of compassion for the situation they found themselves in. "Go ahead in," the man told his family.

Beatrice followed her mother through the door without a backward glance.

Mr. Bailey leaned close to Calvin's ear and whispered, "Come near my daughter again, and you'll wish you had never been born. She's too good for the likes of you. She's leaving Maple Notch as soon as I can arrange transportation." He moved back to a more comfortable distance. "You're right, Mr. Tuttle. This *is* a beautiful day. I will rejoice and be glad in it. Good day to you." He doffed his hat and strode into the sanctuary.

Calvin remained so long in his spot that Tobias had to urge him inside. "Not yet," he said. "Do you remember when Jesus said to make things right with our brother before we bring an offering? Well, something tells me God wouldn't look too kindly on my heart right now."

Peggy hesitated on the front steps.

"You two go on in." Calvin took a step away from the door. "I'll join you later."

The strains of "The Sower" filtered out the door as Calvin turned in the direction of the common. He didn't intend to miss all the service, but for the moment, the anger in his heart kept him from worship. Only God's love could replace that hurt. That's what he could do. Think about good and lovely things—all the things that made God worthy of worship—and not about Mr. Bailey's unreasonable response. He could at least try. As he circled the green, ground he had walked hundreds if not thousands of times in his life, he sought those good and lovely things.

Overhead, a small V of geese honked, heading south toward warmer ground. The first good thing: God protected the geese and all other senseless animals. God would take care of people, too, if only they let Him instead of arguing with their Maker.

The geese came and went with the seasons—another one of God's gifts. This year, the seasons had been odd and off-kilter. Still, for the thousands of years since God gave the promise of the rainbow to Noah, spring had followed winter as surely as year followed year. He thought of the corn ready to harvest in his fields, and the family that would come and assist him in the morning. The stumps had burned to the ground, but smoke pouring out from under the ground assured him that the roots continued to burn. God had given him, Calvin Tuttle, a harvest when many others had none. That was indeed a good thing.

Calvin faced the church. His troubles with Hiram Bailey and his bewitching daughter were far from over, yet he felt at peace, reminded of God's goodness. He slipped into the pew beside Tobias and Peggy as the songmaster lined the next verse of the hymn. Tobias recognized the words from Psalm 23:

"Surely goodness and mercy shall follow me all the days of my life: and I will dwell in the house of the Lord for ever."

Amen, Lord. Amen.

&

Beatrice was supposed to leave Maple Notch, perhaps forever, on Wednesday morning.

Snow started, single flakes falling like a lazy quilter, at dusk on Tuesday evening. Beatrice shrugged on her coat and dashed outside, sticking out her tongue to catch the flakes, letting them settle on her hand to study their intricate beauty before they melted from the heat of her skin. While she stood there, twirling and playing, the snow fell faster, first two flakes, then three, then so many that she could no longer distinguish the individual crystals.

This kind of snowfall usually heralded the beginning of winter in Maple Notch, although it was a few weeks earlier than normal. Of course, nothing about this year had been typical. Had winter ever ended in this Year of our Lord 1816, with freezing temperatures and snowfall at least once every month, including midsummer?

Even after the dreadful year they had experienced, she still loved the lazy, soft, first snowfall. Did it snow like this in New York City? Or did the crowded buildings and grimy streets hide the beauty of a world washed clean by new-fallen snow?

Beatrice told herself Calvin had made a mistake in judgment when he refused her father's offer, but her heart betrayed her. She still loved him. How could she leave Vermont for New York when that meant leaving a part of herself behind?

If it kept snowing like this. . .she might not have to.

Calvin stood in his house, staring out at the snowfall. "Winter's here."

"Did it ever leave?" Tobias asked. In spite of his words of complaint, he was humming to himself. Ever since he had asked for permission to court Peggy, he often had a song on his lips.

At least one of them could hope to find true love.

"It's a good thing we got the corn in." Calvin didn't mention Tobias's cheery mood.

"What? Won't your wonderworking tree stumps clear the field?" Tobias looked up from where he bent over, polishing his boots.

Calvin shook his head in mock frustration. "Don't tell me Burlington's that different. Don't you recognize the first snow of the year when you see it?" Then he grew serious. "Besides, the last snow didn't completely clear. The fires have about burned themselves out, and the weather will stay too cold for the embers to keep the ground thawed." He shoved the bacon to one side of the frying pan and cracked in eggs. "It's a good thing we got all the animals snug in the barn, in case we're snowed in."

Tobias blew out his cheeks and huffed. "If it's that bad, no one will be traveling either."

The fork quivered in Calvin's hand, and he splashed hot grease on his hand. He stuck his hand in a bucket of water and counted to ten under his breath. "Doesn't matter to me."

"Uh-huh." Tobias picked up a piece of harness and began working it. "Tell that to the judge."

Calvin returned to the fry pan. This time he removed the bacon with care and spooned the whites over the tops of the eggs as they browned. "Mr. Bailey won't let me near Bea even if she stays in Maple Notch. It's time I face the truth. Whatever I imagined between us was just that—a figment of my imagination. If she thinks her father's business practices are always fair, then she's not the woman I thought she was."

"Could be she was disappointed when she saw your chance to get ahead fly out the window."

Calvin didn't know how to answer that. He had to focus on Bea's betrayal; otherwise he would hurt too much. In time, he would feel better. If God so willed, he'd find someone else. For now, he had to focus all of his energy on coming up with enough money to pay back Hiram Bailey's bank.

❧

A month later, Calvin's heartache hadn't lessened even one degree, although the temperatures plummeted to new lows. Come Sunday morning, upon arising, he slapped his hands together, seeking warmth. Giving up, he poked among the embers in the fireplace and held his hands over the flames. Good thing they had piled up firewood over the summer. This winter they seemed to use it by the forestfuls. One log would suffice for their morning preparations—no need to waste fuel when they'd be spending most of the forenoon at church.

Behind him, Tobias broke the ice in their water bucket. Next came the sound of a razor scraping against the skin. Calvin shivered. "I told you to let your beard grow out."

"Ah, but Peggy likes my clean-shaven good looks."

Calvin gritted his teeth. To his shame, a part of him begrudged his friend's happiness, but how he longed for his own. "Have you asked for her hand yet?" Not that he had any doubt as to what Peggy's answer would be.

"No." Tobias finished shaving and put away the razor. "There's the minor problem of how I am to support a wife." He grimaced. "And I doubt the local banker would look kindly on granting me a loan to buy land."

"Half of the profit from the crop is yours. It's only right." Calvin spoke from a sense of duty. If he split the profits, could he hope to repay the bank?

Tobias shook his head. "Only if there's anything left over after you pay the bank. That's what we agreed, and I'll hold you to it. Besides, even half the profits won't be enough for me to set up on my own. I'm thinking about returning to work with my father."

Tobias's mouth turned down in a rare frown, and Calvin pushed aside his own worries. Another thought surfaced. "Are you sure you've recovered from your fiancée's death?" Tobias had ended the war with a broken spirit and broken heart, after seeing his mother and sweetheart die.

His friend threw an astonished look at him. "I wouldn't be courting Peggy if my heart wasn't ready. You should know that, my friend."

"But how?" The words traveled from Calvin's heart straight to his mouth, bypassing his brain. Embarrassed, he busied himself pulling on his workday clothes. "I keep telling myself not to spend any more time thinking about what can't be. But my heart keeps drawing me back to Bea." He bent over to fasten his boots.

Tobias straddled the chair he had fashioned and faced Calvin. "I don't know. Give it time. It's only been a month." He ran his hand across the smooth wood of the armrests. "Besides, I have a feeling this isn't the end of things with Miss Bailey. She's still right here in Maple Notch. She hasn't gone anywhere. You still have a chance. . .you just have to decide what you want to do about it."

Calvin opened his mouth to protest, but Tobias spoke again before he could get a word out. "God knows her heart. Keep asking Him for wisdom. He won't lead you astray." He bent over to check the chair legs. "This one turned out well. I think I'll try my hand at making a rocker for Peggy. They say womenfolk like a good rocker."

Calvin accepted the change of topic. *Okay, God, I guess it's up to You. It always has been.* He looked out the window at the white landscape and wished waiting wasn't so hard.

Or so uncertain.

eleven

"I still think you're making a mistake. No one is going out in this weather. Your father says no one has come into the bank all week." Mama fluttered in front of the door as if to bar Beatrice's exit.

"Mama, the church is only around the corner. I'll be fine." No matter how cold it was, Beatrice welcomed the chance to get out of the house. The ladies' mission meeting provided the excuse. "Perhaps next month it will be warmer, and you can come with me."

"Dress warm, then." Mama bundled Beatrice into her coat. Once she opened the door, she found herself grateful for the protection. Thick wool covered every inch of her except for a small space where her eyes peered out over the edge of the scarf. If she needed to dress in this many layers to walk the few feet from her house to the parsonage, would women from the outlying farms attend the meeting? She shivered inside the coat and hurried her steps. *God, please let spring—a real spring—come next year.*

She arrived at the Cabots' home first, and the parson's wife greeted her with a pleasant smile. "Welcome, my dear Miss Bailey." She took care of Beatrice's coat and accessories, then escorted her to a seat and thrust a cup of coffee into her hands. "Do you like sugar with your coffee?"

Nodding, Beatrice studied the familiar room. Sparse furniture crafted with love by members of the congregation dotted the room. Everywhere she looked, she saw signs of the gifts given by the people of the community to their first permanent minister. One simple child's sampler, with an outlined house and chimney and the words "HOME SWEET HOME" caught her attention. "I didn't know you still had that."

"Of course we do. I know how hard you labored over it and how proud you were to give us a gift you had made yourself. That was one of the most precious things we received that year." Mrs. Cabot hugged her. "We'll wait a few minutes, but I fear few will come in light of today's weather." She bustled over to the oven. Beatrice looked around the room again, this time noticing how empty the shelves seemed of food stuffs.

Mrs. Cabot removed a loaf of nut bread from the oven. "It finished just in time. I started on it late this morning, I'm afraid."

Where she had found the ingredients for a special bread, Beatrice couldn't guess. The shelves looked emptier than the fields after harvest. The sweet taste of the sugar in the coffee threatened to gag Beatrice with its wastefulness. She should have taken it black.

Mrs. Cabot cut them each a slice of the bread and served it on a plate. After she sat down, she said, "It appears we will be alone today, but we can still start planning for what the church will do for the needy in our community this Christmas."

"I have some ideas." Beatrice hesitated. Would Mrs. Cabot accept suggestions from someone with so little household management experience? "Since I have little experience stocking a kitchen myself, I asked Cook for her suggestions for staples and quantities and potential costs."

"Very forward thinking of you. You have inherited your father's business acumen."

Startled, Beatrice glanced at Mrs. Cabot but saw only the goodwill of a genuine compliment. The list lay tucked in her muffler. She pulled it out and unrolled the sheets. "Cook made two lists. The first she said included staples—the bare minimum to get by for a family for a month. The second she calls her 'luxury' list—her favorite foodstuffs for special occasions. I had hoped most people would have sufficient staples that we could include a good number of luxuries but"—her hand swept the room—"I would guess many people are living at the edge of starvation this year." Her gaze dropped to her lap, where she rolled up and then straightened out the thin sheets of parchment in her hands, aware that her words might be insulting.

"We have sufficient for our needs, dear Beatrice. God always provides. Let me see." Mrs. Cabot took the pages from her. "I would agree with your cook's assessment. Why don't we compare what we have on hand with her suggestions? I have set up a pantry in the back classroom at the church."

The two women donned their coats and mittens and crossed to the door that connected the house to the church. "Let's work quickly before our fingers are too cold to write," Mrs. Cabot said.

Beatrice stared at the sacks and boxes stacked high in the storage room. "I didn't expect so much."

"After you left, people took your suggestion to heart. Everyone contributed a portion of what they had on hand. God will bless this food, for much of it was truly the gift of the widow's mite."

The parson joined them to assist with moving the heavier items. At the end of an hour, they calculated the results.

"We have enough here for about a month and a half for

every family in Maple Notch. We even have a few of Cook's 'luxury' items."

"People will make it last for at least two months." Parson Cabot spoke cheerfully. "Folks hereabouts can stretch a toothpick until it burns as long as a log. If we're done here, I'll go back to working on my sermon."

They agreed they were finished, and he returned to the church to study while the women returned to the parsonage. Mrs. Cabot poured them coffee, stronger now and even more in need of the sugar, which the parson's wife added without asking. Like the widow's supply of flour and oil, the size of the sugar cone didn't seem to lessen. Beatrice smiled at the fanciful thought.

"Enough for two months. More, since not everyone will need help. That's good, isn't it?"

Mrs. Cabot stirred some milk into her coffee. "There's fewer that will be asking than will be in need. We want to give a basket to every family in the church at Christmas so we don't hurt anyone's pride."

Every family. "Is it really that terrible?"

"It is." Mrs. Cabot nodded. "We'll keep some foodstuffs here, so that those in the most desperate circumstances can seek us out. But let me assure you, the supplies will be welcome in every household."

Enough for two months. January and February. "That still leaves half a year or more until the next harvest. If. . .if people run out, what will they do?"

"Eat what they can catch or kill. Survive, like the Pilgrims did that first winter at Plymouth. Mr. Dixon has agreed to carry accounts on credit if the need arises. And we'll all trust God for a better growing season in 1817."

The realities struck Beatrice as she walked home not much later. *"Dixon will have to charge more than they can afford. They'll need to borrow the money. . .from your father's bank."* Calvin's words haunted her. The people of Maple Notch couldn't afford to pay high prices for seed.

Not when they didn't even have the money to buy food.

❧

Christmas Eve had arrived, providing a welcome break in the monotony of winter days. In a few minutes, Calvin and Tobias would make their way to Uncle Stephen's house for a celebration that would continue into tomorrow. Solomon and his family would join them. The two households had traded hosting holidays for as long as Calvin could remember. One day, he hoped he, too, could host their family gatherings.

"Not much chance of that." He looked around his tiny cabin. They didn't even have chairs enough for the adults to sit, nor space to place them if people brought their own. *I'll make it bigger next year.* Why did everything always have to be next year?

"What's that?" Tobias checked the presents they had bundled into a large bag.

"Talking to myself." Calvin grinned. "Too bad that rocking chair won't fit in the sack."

"It's in the barn. Mr. Reid is keeping it a secret until the big day."

"That's a serious present, you know. As good as—"

"I know. You don't have to tell me. I would. I will. . . ." The two men exchanged a look. "As soon as I can."

"If I know my cousin, she doesn't care about having a lot of things. She'll be happy most anywhere as long as she's with you."

"Tell that to her father." They grinned at each other. They both knew Stephen would agree to the wedding whenever Tobias asked.

"It's a good thing we have a sled to help us carry everything. We'd never make it on our own." In the spirit of the season, he began to sing "O Come, All Ye Faithful."

A knock sounded on the door.

"Company?" Tobias lifted his eyebrows as he headed for the door. "Parson! Mrs. Cabot, Miss Bailey. Come in."

Miss Bailey. Before the words could register on Calvin's consciousness, she had entered the room, her face full of beaming good will, her eyes pleading for—what? Understanding?

Belatedly, he remembered his manners and took off his hat. "Sit down and stay awhile. Would you like some tea?"

"Don't mind if I do." Parson Cabot settled on one of the sturdy Windsor chairs Tobias had made that fall. His hand brushed against the bag of gaily wrapped presents. "I see you were heading out for Christmas. We won't keep you long, but I'm glad we caught you." He handed a bundle of his own to Calvin.

Calvin unwound the string around the sack and peered inside. On top lay sacks of beans, flour, and a cone of sugar. "What's this for? We didn't ask. . ."

"No, but we are redistributing the food people brought to the church last summer. That was Miss Bailey's idea." He nodded at Bea, who turned red. "Everyone in the community will receive a part, even the ones who don't come to church except for marrying and burying."

"We can't take this. Save it for families. . . ." His voice trailed. He saw the steely look in Bea's eyes and the pastoral concern in the parson's.

"We only wish it were more." Beatrice's soft voice held undercurrents he couldn't decipher.

"Tobias, would you be so kind as to show me that rocking chair everyone's talking about? I've thought of asking you to make one for the wife." Mr. and Mrs. Cabot followed Tobias out the door, leaving Calvin alone with Bea.

"Was this your idea?" he asked in a strangled voice. "Just because I refused your father's offer doesn't make me a pauper in need of charity."

"The Cabots suggested giving food to every family in the community, although I wish I had thought of it."

A sheen of tears glimmered in her eyes, and he steeled himself against it. She walked around his house, her mittened hands touching his things, her gaze lingering on the shelf above the table where they kept basic supplies. The single room was functional but lacked those feminine touches that made a home. He wondered how it looked to her.

When at last she looked at him again, she had composed herself. "You are indeed well stocked compared to some homes we have visited. Some people have less than you do, for a family of six, seven, even more. I only wish we could do more."

What had happened to the woman with the let-them-eat-cake attitude? Voice husky, he said, "Then give them what you intended for us. We have enough to make do. The first settlers here survived on less."

She shook her head. "That would embarrass folks if they found out."

He thought on the problem. "But if we should bring a gift, privately, for the food pantry?"

A smile sneaked around her lips. "That might be acceptable.

But please, keep this gift if you or any in your family can use it. Don't let your pride get in your way."

The teakettle whistled, and he realized she was still standing in her coat. He helped her out of it and led her to a chair. "Would you care for some tea?"

The small smile returned. "Didn't you say you were on your way to a Christmas celebration? And my parents are expecting me back soon." She pulled off her mittens and ran her finger along the smooth finish of the chair, but the expression on her face looked sad. "Please don't think less of me for wanting to respect their wishes." She glanced out the window. "Before the Cabots come back in, I want to say something." She spoke in a rush. "You were right. I see that now."

The door opened with her last word, cutting off any response he might have wished to make.

Their guests left a few minutes later, and the first stars were coming out as Calvin crossed the fields to Uncle Stephen's house with Tobias. They shone stark and bright against the darkening sky. He couldn't get Bea's last words, as she left with the Cabots, out of his mind.

"Let this be a season of peace and goodwill between us." She said it so only he could hear, and pressed her hand against his sleeve. Now he touched the spot where her hand had rested, still feeling the burn through the layers to his skin.

A new season of goodwill. Was such a thing possible?

Had God answered his prayer at last?

❧

"The weather couldn't be any more perfect for a winter frolic!"

Papa had reluctantly agreed to let Peggy Reid spend the night with Beatrice in anticipation of the young people's party. The two young women looked out through the window at the clear blue sky, sparkling over a thick covering of snow on the ground.

"You'd think it was perfect weather even if the snow turned to slush and the sleds would bump down the hill over rocks," Beatrice said.

"Would not." But Peggy giggled.

"Why don't you admit it? You've been walking in the clouds ever since Tobias gave you that rocking chair for Christmas."

Peggy's giggle turned into outright laughter. "And yesterday was Valentine's Day."

"And a certain Tobias Heath just came back from Burlington. I know." The lighthearted banter fell flat on Beatrice's heart. If only she could be this excited about the day.

"Is your father still set against Calvin?" Peggy asked sympathetically, the giggle gone from her voice.

Beatrice nodded, glum. "I'm glad he's out of town this weekend, or else he might have changed his mind at the last minute and forbidden me to go to the frolic. He's convinced everyone wants to get me and Calvin together."

"Sh!" Peggy put her finger to her lips. "Don't tell anyone, but we do."

"Breakfast is ready," Cook called up the stairs.

The two women headed for the stairs. "I don't know if I'd ever get used to a house like this." Peggy lifted the hem of her skirt and descended a step. "Enough rooms to fill two stories plus an attic. Imagine."

"I'm sure there are plenty of houses like this in Burlington. They're just not as practical for a farmer." Beatrice tried to make light of the difference.

Peggy shrugged it off. "Something smells heavenly. I'd be

as big as a moose if I ate here every day. How do you stay so slender?"

"It's easy when you don't have much of an appetite." Beatrice meant the statement as humorous repartee, but when Cook placed an egg cup in front of her, her stomach rebelled. Feeling the watchful gaze of three women—Mama, as well as Peggy and Cook—Beatrice made herself slice off the top of the egg and season the yolk and white left inside. Somehow she managed to get it down between bites of toast and generous helpings of tea. She made it last while Peggy went through bacon and oatmeal in addition to her eggs.

"Do you want to take a warming stone with you?" Cook fussed. " 'Twill be awful cold out there."

Beatrice imagined pushing a warming stone along with her skates, a small puddle trailing behind her on the ice. The image brought a smile to her lips. "We'll be too busy having fun to get cold. But thank you."

By midmorning when the worst of the nighttime chill had passed, they headed out the door for the church. Once the door closed behind them, Peggy said, "You might have fooled your mother, but you didn't fool me. You only picked at your breakfast." She clucked under her breath. "Someone has to get you and Calvin together before you waste away. And I have an idea."

"Miss Bailey!"

Beatrice's head whipped around at the sound of the familiar voice. Calvin. Even muffled as he was beneath scarf and rabbit skin hat, his brown eyes gleamed with mischief and happiness. Or was she imagining he shared her happiness at being together again? Aside from quick, formal greetings at church, they hadn't spoken since their all-too-brief visit on

Christmas Eve. Papa had made sure of that.

"Smile." Peggy whispered in her ear.

Beatrice did better than that. She slipped a mittened hand out of her muffler and waved. Calvin made as if to run to her across the common, but his legs sank to his knees in the snow. He shrugged, stood, and walked on the road around the corner. While she waited for him to draw close, several other young people arrived at the common. The air rang with the greetings and good humor of people released from their midwinter doldrums. When Calvin took her arm at the same time Tobias took Peggy's, it felt natural and right.

Tobias and Peggy fell back, allowing Calvin and Beatrice the illusion of privacy. Even with two dozen people milling around the church yard, Beatrice felt encapsulated in their own snowball, hidden from view to all but God.

"I feared I wouldn't see you today, that your father might forbid it." Calvin's voice sounded low, tender.

"He's out of town." She couldn't keep the smile away from her lips. "I told Mama I was coming, and she didn't speak against it."

Beside her, Calvin stiffened. What had she said to offend him now?

"I don't want to sneak behind his back." Calvin held himself rigid. "I'm still not good enough for him."

"Would you rather not see me at all?" What was wrong with the man? "The question isn't what my father thinks of you but what *I* think of you."

His hold on her arm tightened, then she felt it relax, one fingertip at a time. "Oh, Beatrice Alice Bailey, what I am to do with you? You keep bringing me back to what is important." His mouth opened in a crooked grin. "Let's gather rosebuds while we may, for old time—and your father—will be a-flying."

"I didn't take you for the poetic type," Beatrice said.

"My mother's prized book of poetry." The scowl that had darkened his face cleared, and a genuine smile broke through, as warm as the sun high in the sky. "Let's go lace on our skates."

⁂

Parson Cabot had done a good job creating the skating pond, Calvin decided. Although numerous bodies of water across the Notch froze over during the winter, all of them posed difficulties. Often rocks and other debris frozen in the ice posed a threat. So when the church held a skating party, the pastor worked on creating an artificial pond behind the church. In the sunshine, it looked as clear as the floor of crystal in the New Jerusalem.

Last year Calvin had enjoyed the skating frolic, his first since he returned from the war. How much more he looked forward to this year, with Bea on his arm. He glanced down at her, her brown eyes alight with merriment, and the remainder of his hesitation about the day took flight.

He led her to a large boulder. "Let me help you fit your skates over your boots." Removing his mittens, he took the pair of metal blades made to fit her feet perfectly. They flashed with nearly new sparkle, finer than anything he had ever worn to skate. One Christmas, his parents had invested in metal blades when he had begged for them. He had swapped out the soles for larger ones as he outgrew the original pair, and he continued to use them, taking care that he didn't wobble and fall. With good maintenance, annual sharpening, and care wearing them, he expected them to last for his lifetime.

At least they were made of metal. Glancing around at the other young people confirmed several of them still used runners fashioned from animal bones.

He tightened the blades on Beatrice's small feet and checked them. "Is that comfortable?"

She stood. "Perfect." She glanced at the ice, longing in her eyes.

"Go on ahead. I'll join you on the ice in a minute." He didn't know that he wanted her to watch him attach his outgrown skates to his boots.

"Don't want me to see you trip over your own two feet?" Her smile let him know she was teasing. "I'm not going anywhere."

He looked at the blades in his hands. If they were to have a future together, she'd have to accept things as they were, the make-do reality of his life, not as they might wish them to be. Bending over, he pulled the loop tight against his right boot.

"These look like you've enjoyed many good times in them." He glanced up to see her turning the extra blade over in her hand. "I haven't had many opportunities to skate aside from parties held at church. Too dangerous, both Mama and Papa agreed." She looked longingly at the simple skate in her lap.

He finished with the fastenings and reached for the second blade. Their gazes caught, locked together.

"You may think my family is rich." She glanced away at the spot where Peggy headed onto the ice with Tobias. "But your family is rich in memories. I know which one I'd prefer."

Calvin's heart went to his head, leaving him senseless, and he couldn't have said whether he fastened the second skate on securely or not. The next thing he knew, he was on the ice with Beatrice. The two of them glided together as if they had done it all their lives, in perfect harmony—the way a couple should be. Had they skated together before? He searched for a memory.

"Do you remember the skating party we had, maybe a year or so before the war?"

Was she reading his mind? "Yes." He could picture her still: Peggy's constant companion, a shy young beauty even then, with glistening golden hair.

She giggled. "You were so grown up. I was longing to skate with you, but you didn't even know I existed except as Peggy's friend."

"And she asked me to skate with you." The memory cleared now. All he had wanted to do was to skate with Hannah White. Strange how all that had changed. At the time, he was certain his future lay with Hannah, but she had married while he was gone to war and had turned into a nagging housewife from what he had heard. God had spared him.

"And you graciously agreed to your pesky cousin's request and made me very happy indeed."

"I remember." He smiled at the memory. "You talked with me about how Parson Cabot enlarged the pond the summer before and what you had read in the almanac about the chances for the year's crops. You sounded like a right young farmer. At least until you quoted poetry at me." She had driven Hannah White out of his mind, at least temporarily.

Her cheeks brightened. "I was so thrilled that you were taking me seriously. I felt very grown up that day." Luminous brown eyes peeked out from beneath her bonnet. "You're doing it all over again."

The way she looked at him, adoration shining in her eyes, took all his willpower not to lean over and kiss the inviting lips. He wouldn't do that again, not here, not anywhere, until some things changed. He must speak his mind. He turned around, skating backward while holding on to her hands. "You know I care deeply for you."

"Yes?" She looked at him with such hope in her eyes that he hated what he must say next.

"And I believe you feel the same way about me." He held his breath. What if she said no?

She nodded, her cheeks blazing red.

"But your father has forbidden our courtship. Is it right for us to continue without his blessing?"

Her eyes widened at the sight of something behind him, out of his sight. Before he turned, he knew whom he would see.

Hiram Bailey.

twelve

Parson Cabot skated to the couple with an agility surprising in a man of his age. "Calvin, Beatrice, I suggest you head to the parsonage. I will speak with Mr. Bailey."

Calvin tugged Beatrice's hand. "Can you walk in your blades?" She nodded, and they hobbled across the snow toward the back door of the parsonage.

"Good day, Mr. Bailey." Parson Cabot intercepted Papa in time to let them escape inside.

Beatrice collapsed on the closest chair, her whole body trembling. Her face felt frozen, as much from fear as from cold. "What are we to do?"

"How good to see you both today." Mrs. Cabot greeted them as if having people barge into her house with their skates on happened every day. "Would you like some tea?"

Shaking her head, Beatrice took off her coat and bent over to unfasten the blades. Calvin did the same.

"Don't worry, my dears. My husband will calm Mr. Bailey down before he brings him to the house." Mrs. Cabot handed a piece of still-steaming gingerbread into Calvin's hands. "It might be best if Calvin leaves now." Her suggestion was in reality a command, and they both knew it.

Calvin glanced at the door as if expecting it to burst open, then back at Beatrice, uncertainty written on his features.

"Go," Beatrice encouraged. "Let us pray as though our lives depended on it."

His shoulders stiffened, his manly pride fighting with his common sense.

"Sometimes it is better to retreat and fight your battle another day. My husband will speak with Mr. Bailey. Go in peace."

"Until we meet again." Calvin didn't waste more time arguing. He disappeared out the covered walkway that connected the parsonage with the church. Beatrice stared at the closed door, wondering if the impediments to a relationship between them would always remain so firmly in place.

"Do you wish me to speak for you, dear?" Mrs. Cabot's voice intruded on her thoughts. "Sometimes it is easier to ask someone outside the family to soothe troubled waters."

Beatrice could hear the nervousness in her laughter. "I feel like we're Romeo and Juliet or Hero and Leander. I don't think there's anything you could say to Papa to change his mind about Calvin."

"But you love him, don't you?" The same sweet voice that had comforted Beatrice when she had fallen down during a race at the church picnic as a child invited confidences now.

"Oh yes, Mrs. Cabot. I do."

Boots stamped on the ground outside, heralding the arrival of the two men. "Then that's all I need to know." Mrs. Cabot opened the door. "Welcome, Mr. Bailey. Please do come in."

Beatrice brushed down her skirt. Not a single water stain smudged the perfect lay of her dress, as spotless as the day had been. She raised her chin. She had done nothing shameful.

"Beatrice." Papa's voice hung on a razor's edge between conciliation and anger.

"Papa. You must have had good success in Burlington to return so promptly."

His eyes flared, and she knew she had spoken amiss. "You weren't expecting me to return in time to see you skating with Mr. Tuttle."

She refused to let him shame her. "I told Mama about the skating frolic."

"But not about Mr. Tuttle." Papa refused to back down.

"We did not plan to meet, if that is what you are implying."

"Please, Mr. Bailey. Sit down. Have a cup of tea and some gingerbread." Mrs. Cabot shoved a cup in his hands before he could refuse it. He took the chair opposite Beatrice, his dark eyes matching hers stare for stare.

"I have told Mr. Bailey that both you and Calvin were in my sight the entire time and that nothing untoward happened. You appeared to be enjoying a few pleasant turns on the ice." In a burst of unwelcome honesty, the parson added, "And perhaps to discuss a few matters of concern to you both."

"I must accept the parson's word about what transpired between you." Papa spoke directly to Beatrice. "But I will not suffer that young farmer to speak against me. What did he say?"

"Surely that is a private matter between the two young people," Mrs. Cabot said.

"He said"—Beatrice raised her voice over Mrs. Cabot's objection—"that no matter what his feelings toward me may be, he refused to ask me to act against your wishes." Her voice came close to breaking into tears.

"That is well." Papa stared at the tea cup in his hand as if ready to throw it against the fireplace. "These are my wishes. I forbid you to speak to him or see him again. The man is not fit to be the husband of my daughter." He returned the cup to Mrs. Cabot. "I'm afraid I have no taste for tea this afternoon. Come, Beatrice, we are finished here."

"Do you object to my spending time with Mrs. Cabot?" Beatrice felt a temper equal to that of her father rising.

"What? You wish to stay?"

She nodded.

"Will you promise me that they won't use your home as a meeting place?" Papa turned to the parson. Beatrice shrank inside herself. No one should address their pastor in that tone of voice.

Mrs. Cabot nodded at the parson. "You have my promise." Although he said the words, he didn't appear happy.

"Very well. I will expect a man of the cloth to keep his word. And, Beatrice, I will know when the skating party has ended—I will expect you home right after." His back as rigid as Calvin's had been earlier, Papa marched through the door.

Once he had left, Mrs. Cabot walked across the room and opened the doorway to the church. Beatrice rose. Had Calvin been standing there the whole time? Would the Cabots allow them to meet in spite of the promise the parson had given?

Mrs. Cabot returned with Peggy, both of them wreathed in smiles. "I know you promised not to speak or meet with Calvin." Her friend's attempt to look serious failed, and she giggled.

"I fail to see anything funny about it." Beatrice accepted Mrs. Cabot's handkerchief and dabbed at the tears spilling from her eyes.

"Cheer up." Peggy handed a quill and paper to Beatrice. "You didn't promise not to *write* to him."

As Peggy explained their plan, even Beatrice's face lifted in a smile.

❧

"How much corn did Rusk say he wanted?" Tobias asked.

"What's that?" Calvin stared at Bea's latest letter that Peggy had delivered that afternoon.

"Never mind." Tobias bent over the sheet of paper where they had recorded requests for seed corn. "You won't pay attention to me until you've read every word on that page at least a dozen times and committed them to memory."

Calvin grunted in agreement. His friend understood him well enough. Every day that passed without a letter felt like a year had passed. If he thought he loved Bea before, that love had flared into something rarer, finer, as he had seen deep into her soul through their correspondence. She detailed life as seen through her window, such as the fight of the tiny chickadees and the lowly sparrow to survive Vermont's harsh winter and the first signs that this year perhaps, indeed, spring would arrive.

They had agreed to read the same passages of the Bible every day—five Psalms and one chapter of Proverbs. So far they had read through both books twice. As they shared their thoughts, his love for the Lord grew in conjunction with his admiration for Bea. She was a woman whose value was above rubies, whose husband could trust in her.

"Have faith."

It took a moment for Calvin to realize Tobias had said the words, because he had read them so often in Bea's letters.

"I believe God will bring things together for all of us this spring. Peggy and I, you and Beatrice."

Calvin set down the paper. "From your lips to God's ears. I

pray it is so." He found the place Tobias had marked on the ledger. "Whitson wants five bushels?"

"He's even offered us more money if we'll sell him extra."

Calvin shook his head. "One times one is still one. We can't make more than we have. I hope we have enough to sell everyone what they need, and if we're lucky, we'll have extra. Do we have a total yet?"

"We haven't heard from Frisk or the Johnsons, but of course they both salvaged some of their crops. They may not want to buy any from us." Tobias ticked the end of the pencil against his teeth.

Calvin ran his finger down the list. "Some have asked for more than they should need. Maybe they're afraid of another year like last year."

"Let's pray not." Tobias managed a lopsided grin. "You don't have any more stumps to burn out."

"If it happens again, I suspect the whole town will pack up and move south." Calvin looked at the numbers. "And some people have requested a bare minimum."

"Think it's a matter of how much money people can afford?"

Calvin shrugged. "I'm thinking about setting a limit. Two bushels of corn per farm if they're asking to buy. Including my own family. A dollar a bushel, the same price for everyone. That way everybody gets treated the same way. It hurts my head to think about who might need it more or less."

Tobias lifted his eyebrows at that. "You really don't want to make money on this, do you?"

"It feels wrong to profit from other people's tragedy." Calvin sucked in his lips and totaled the names on the page. "Twenty, twenty-three including our three family farms." He made a mark on the page. "And I might see about selling whatever is left to the mercantile over in St. Albans. They must be facing the same problems we are." He rolled his shoulders to ease out the kinks formed from huddling over the books for so long. "Come on, let's get outside. I'm going to see if Solomon will let me borrow his wagon."

"How about your uncle?" Tobias's grin gave away his thoughts.

"You just want to see Peggy," Calvin said.

"Anything wrong with that?"

Calvin's glance fell on the latest letter from Bea. Maybe they didn't need to leave right away. "Nothing. Nothing at all." He took a seat and pulled a fresh sheet of paper toward him. Dipping his quill in ink, he wrote *"Dearest Bea. . ."*

❧

"The plans I have set in motion for the sale of my seed corn will provide enough money to repay my debt to your father's bank." Once again, Beatrice moved her cat off the letter so she could read Calvin's message.

The door to Beatrice's room swung open and she folded the page into the sleeve of her dressing gown. Bessie entered, bearing a ewer of warm water. She glanced at the sleeve of Beatrice's dress, where a white corner dangled.

"Did you hear from Mr. Tuttle again?" Bessie whispered as she poured water into the basin on the bed stand, where it steamed in the cool air.

Beatrice glanced at the door, fearful one of her parents might overhear.

"Mr. and Mrs. Bailey are in the drawing room downstairs. The mistress thought you might want to freshen up before the dinner party tonight."

Beatrice had enlisted her maid's help in corresponding with Calvin. So far, no one had guessed. Neither parent had forbidden it, but she had no doubt they would if they ever learned about it. She nodded. "I want to read the letter before I go downstairs."

"I'll tell your mother you need a few more minutes." Bessie winked at Beatrice. "Use the time any way you want to." She slipped out the door.

"If only I could avoid this dinner altogether." Papa seemed determined to introduce her to every eligible suitor within a fifty-mile radius. Tonight she was to entertain Reginald Perkins, the widowed owner of the emporium in nearby St. Albans. He was a man of at least thirty, with the appearance of a jolly peddler, if she remembered him correctly. She shuddered at the thought. A pleasant man, good with his customers, kind and a good friend—but would she want him as a husband? He held no interest for her.

Beatrice had already dressed as much as she intended to for the visit, donning one of the dresses they had had made during her stay in New York. Mama had asked her to wear the rose dress, but Beatrice couldn't bring herself to do that. Calvin favored her in pink, and she wore it to church if at all. There he could at least see her, even if they couldn't speak. The curls Bessie had helped style in her hair remained in place. With the extra few minutes the maid promised, Beatrice could cherish the rest of the letter.

Once I have satisfied the debt and we are on even terms,
I will renew my request for permission to court you properly.
Pray that your father receives me with kindness.

Oh, could it be? Beatrice hardened herself against the tears that wanted to flow. If she went down to dinner with red-rimmed eyes, Mama would ask questions. How she longed to sit down and dash off a reply, but Bessie couldn't buy that much time for her. Instead, she settled for a second reading of the letter, committing much of it to memory before she hid it in a box with pressed leaves and other childish mementoes she stored in her armoire.

After that, Beatrice put on her most important adornment—an interested smile—and went downstairs to greet Mr. Perkins.

The sight of the man waiting for her in the drawing room might have made her laugh in different circumstances. Mr. Perkins almost looked like a dandy. Had he ordered new clothing for tonight's dinner? If only she could feel any degree of interest in the man. In the flickering candlelight, set atop the table although twilight still shone through the windows, he looked eager, almost boyish, the lighting doing kind things to his eyes, erasing wrinkles, and revealing only his good humor.

"Miss Bailey. How lovely to see you again." He bowed in her direction. She offered her hand, and he kissed it. His voice was strong. She could imagine him calling orders across his store, or perhaps telling an engaging tale to his children.

He had a number of admirable qualities, but she felt nothing when she looked at him except possible friendship.

"It didn't matter where that mother cat took her kittens, Mandy always caught up with her. Eventually she gave up." Mr. Perkins finished a story about his youngest daughter.

Beatrice's guess had proved correct; he loved telling stories, especially about his three offspring. She could picture the three lonely children through his eyes: sweet, not perfect, but well behaved and healthy.

"Do you like children, Miss Bailey?" Mr. Perkins addressed the question to her.

Beatrice's heart sped at the personal question. How could she answer? If she said yes. . .but if she said no. . .

When she hesitated, Papa's lips tightened in the beginnings of a frown. "Of course she does." He wrapped his fingers around the coffee cup waiting by his plate. "How has business been? Has this year without a summer made it difficult?"

Once again, Beatrice squirmed. Between Mr. Perkins's question about children and Papa asking about business, she felt like she was sitting in on a bargaining session for her hand.

"Not too bad. A few people have purchased things on account, but I'm certain this year shall see improvement. By year's end, I expect to turn a tidy profit. Yes, indeed." He settled back against his chair and looked at Papa with the confidence of a successful man of business. "My family is well provided for." He looked meaningfully at Beatrice.

With the right man, I'd be happy with a sack of beans and a handful of cornmeal. But Beatrice knew better than to voice her thoughts aloud.

"In fact, a good piece of business has come my way recently." Mr. Perkins beamed, oblivious to Beatrice's indifference to his financial health. "I've found a source of seed corn to sell to our locals. Someone from your neck of the woods, in fact. You may know him—Calvin Tuttle?"

❧

"Looks like we have company," Tobias called out.

Calvin glanced up from where he plied his hoe to sift

through the ashes from the tree roots. Here and there he found small chunks that needed to be dug out. By the time they finished, the amount of arable land would have nearly doubled.

His heart clenched when he saw their unexpected guest. *Hiram Bailey.* Calvin looked down at his stained breeches, his dirt-encrusted hands. *So be it. And God, give me the words to say.* The two men hadn't spoken since the day of the skating frolic, not even at Sunday services. Had he discovered the correspondence with Beatrice?

Bailey pulled up his horse. "Mr. Tuttle. May I have a word with you?"

In a low voice, Tobias said, "I'm praying." Calvin nodded and walked across the field toward his nemesis.

"Mr. Bailey. What brings you out here on this fine spring day?" Calvin matched the banker's even tones.

"I have a business matter I'd like to discuss with you. May we go to your cabin?" Bailey remained astride his horse. Calvin wondered if the height was meant to intimidate him. He refused to let that happen.

"I'm sorry, Mr. Bailey, but we are in the midst of spring planting, as you can see. I hope to come in to the bank later this month regarding the loan."

Bailey frowned, as if unsettled that Calvin controlled the timing of their discussion. "That's not what I came about. I heard you are selling your seed corn to the storekeeper in St. Albans." He waited, as if expecting an answer to an unasked question.

"That is correct."

Bailey pulled on his horse's reins but loosened them when the horse whinnied its protest. "If you have extra seed corn, I am still interested in buying it. For six dollars a bushel. Come now. You can't complain. You've made your point and played Joseph to the people of Maple Notch."

Calvin held his tongue.

"People elsewhere will buy the corn, no matter the price. Why not accept a transaction that benefits us both?" Bailey took off his riding gloves and slapped them against his bulging pocket.

The sweat on Calvin's back turned to ice water, chilling him to the bone. "My answer remains unchanged. No matter where they live, farmers are my neighbors just as the man on the Jericho Road was the Samaritan's neighbor. I can't accept such a high price." *Have I just said good-bye to this man's blessing on my courtship of his daughter. . .again?* "I will sell it to you for the same price I've charged everyone else. One dollar a bushel."

Bailey's face turned pale before it darkened into a deep red of rage. "Very well. I had hoped that you had gained some common sense over the winter, but I was wrong. I shall expect your payment in full in a week's time." He turned his horse around and galloped in the direction of the river.

"Why not take the man's money, if he's so anxious to give it away?" Tobias asked. "It's not like you have that much corn left over."

Calvin turned a murderous glare on him, and Tobias backed off. "Because it's wrong."

Calvin stopped paying attention. Bailey had run off, his horse at full gallop, and a sense of impending danger urged him to action. He stood debating the wisdom of going for his own mount when he heard a scream coming from the direction of the river.

thirteen

"Get blankets and meet me at the bridge." Calvin hollered at Tobias as he sprinted in the direction of the scream.

Lord, let me get there in time. Calvin didn't know what to expect. A few feet shy of the bridge, he slowed down his pace to avoid the same fate he feared had befallen Bailey.

Calvin surveyed the scene in front of him with mounting panic. On the opposite side of the river, Bailey's horse stood some distance from the riverbank, its sides heaving and shuddering in near panic.

The middle of the bridge, where they had replaced planks last year, had broken, a gaping hole where solid wood should be.

Of Hiram Bailey—no sign was visible.

Calvin dismounted and took a cautious step onto the bridge, then another. The wood at the near end of the bridge seemed solid enough for his weight.

"What are you doing?" Tobias spoke from the embankment.

"Looking for Mr. Bailey." He peered over the edge of the hole, fearful he might see a body impaled on one of the broken pilings, but he found no sign of him. "Mr. Bailey?" Calvin shielded his eyes from the sun glinting off the running water and looked downstream. If the river carried him. . . He shuddered to think about the rocks and other obstacles that lay along that route. If the man had worn a hunter's red jacket or even a mustard yellow, he would be easier to spot against the dark water and woods and rock.

"I see something."

Calvin turned in the direction Tobias pointed—a patch of blue wool had snagged on lichen-covered rock on the near side of the riverbank. They both crashed through the woods toward the rock. Faint moans reached them when they were a few yards away.

"He's alive!" Relief gave speed to Calvin's legs, and he smashed through branches to the side of the river. Bailey clung to a large boulder at the edge of the water, but his fingers looked blue and numb and ready to let go.

"We're coming, Mr. Bailey. Hold on."

"Give me the rope." Calvin called to Tobias as he pulled off his coat. Anything heavy or bulky would only hinder him. He moved cautiously, planting his feet on the slippery rock, finding a foothold and securing his weight before letting go of the tree leaning over the river.

Bailey's fingers loosened their grip on the lichen-covered rock. "Oh no you don't." Calvin grabbed the man by the elbows and pulled him onto the rock beside him. Bailey was saying something, but Calvin couldn't distinguish the words straining through his chattering teeth.

First problem solved. Now how did he get both of them back onto the bank where Tobias waited with the rope? "Throw one end to me."

Tobias did as he requested, and Calvin tied a knot around Bailey's waist. Maybe a foot, half a yard at most, separated the rock from the creek bank, but it might as well have been a mile with Bailey's inert weight. The man might not survive another plunge into the icy river water.

Tobias spotted the same problem. He found a stone wedged

into the exposed riverbank and tested his weight on it. It held, and he climbed down to lean across the empty space. He had closed the distance by half. It would have to do.

Head or feet first? Feet, Calvin decided. If they did lose their hold and Bailey slipped into the water, better it be his feet.

Balancing himself on the edge of the large boulder, Calvin took Bailey in his arms and leaned toward where Tobias stood at the edge of the water. Slowly, slowly, he moved his arms up Bailey's torso, feeding his feet and legs toward Tobias.

"Got 'im!" Tobias called. He pulled Bailey's legs over his shoulder, until the banker looked like a fish ready to slide into the water. He gestured with his hand. *Keep him coming.*

Calvin watched Bailey's feet inch up the river bank until at last the man's head fell from his hands and almost threw him off balance. Tobias held Bailey in his arms.

"Wish I could paint a picture of this. If he survives." Calvin reached for the riverbank with one long leg and landed with a *whoosh* next to Tobias.

The two friends squatted beside the banker to make an assessment. At least he was out of the water. Before they did anything else, Calvin ran his hands up and down Bailey's arms and legs for broken bones. "I think his left leg is broken below the knee," he told Tobias. Rib cage next. Bailey moaned.

"Broken ribs, too?" Tobias asked.

"I'm no expert." Calvin probed Bailey's chest as gently as he could. "I don't think anything else is broken, but I'm sure he'll be bruised all over. We need to make a litter. The sooner we get him warm. . ."

They made quick work of constructing the litter out of

two logs and a blanket, and trotted back to the cabin with their burden. "Go ahead to Uncle Stephen's. Tell him what's happened, and ask him to come as soon as possible." Tobias left the yard, and Calvin picked Bailey up. He stretched the man out on his feather tick, removed his wet clothes, and covered him with a quilt.

Next, he built up the fire and set a kettle of water on to heat. The door behind him opened as he returned to examine Bailey's injuries.

"How bad is he?" Uncle Stephen joined him at the bedside and studied the prone figure. "All you can do is keep him quiet and warm, since there's no doctor nearby."

"That's what I thought." After his battle experience, Calvin knew the best course of action was to wait and see if infection set in. He would pray that didn't happen, because then amputation might be the only answer. "Do you mind staying here while I go to town and let his family know?"

"Of course." Uncle Stephen waved the question away. "Tobias will return in a few minutes with Hilda and Peggy. He'll have more attention than he may want."

"I don't know how long I'll be."

"Doesn't matter. Now go. They may already be worried about him at the bank."

Calvin climbed on his horse one more time and cantered past his fields, where the hoe lay abandoned in the soil. Tobias would take care of it. Funny how the importance of planting dimmed when a man's life lay in the balance. If Mr. Bailey usually returned home for his luncheon, Beatrice and her mother would expect him at any moment. Calvin had no time to lose.

Should he take the horse through the water or head north

to the nearest bridge? Due to spring runoff, the water was running high, and the current was strong at the spot they had built the bridge. He wouldn't attempt the crossing there, but at the shallows about a mile upstream. The horse made his way across easily enough. Minutes later, they reached the road into town and raced onward.

Ahead of him, he saw the town common. The sun beat down on his neck, indicating high noon. He pulled up in front of the house, tied the horse to a maple tree, and ran to the door, pounding his fist against the solid oak.

Bea herself answered the door.

※

"Calvin?" Beatrice blinked, not quite believing his presence on her doorstep. Had he spoken to her father already? Was the news good? A smile forced its way from her heart onto her face.

"Who is it, dear?" Mama's voice intruded.

"Please let me in." Whatever emotion Calvin's voice held, it didn't sound like happiness, and his clothes were damp. She opened the door wide enough for him to come in and called to her mother over her shoulder. "It's"—she stopped herself from saying "Calvin" in the nick of time—"Mr. Tuttle."

Footsteps hurried down the corridor, and Mama met them in the front hall, a faint frown on her face. She, too, saw something in Calvin's expression that made her pause. "I think you had best come in, Mr. Tuttle, and tell us your business."

Even as distraught as Calvin was, Beatrice drank in the sight, sound, smell of him. Fresh air and hard work, clothing stained... none of it mattered. He had taken off his hat and stood with his feet planted apart, a solid man from head to toe.

"It's Mr. Bailey. He came to see me this morning."

Beatrice let out an involuntary cry. Had Papa found out about their secret correspondence? Calvin caught her cry and shook his head.

"Did you argue?" Mama's lips returned to their straight, unhappy line.

"That's not why I'm here." He looked at the floor, then around the room, and finally returned his gaze to the two of them. "The truth is, the bridge gave way when he attempted the crossing, and he fell in."

Mama gasped, and she clutched Beatrice's arm. A lifetime of possibilities crossed her mind.

"We—Mr. Heath and I—fished him out of the water and took him to my house. My uncle is with him now."

"Is he—?" Beatrice hesitated to ask.

"His leg is broken, but nothing else appears to be broken. Tobias and I agreed the best thing for him is to stay put and rest."

"He needs a doctor." Mama fidgeted. "How can we get word to the doctor down in Burlington?"

"Take us to him." Beatrice trusted Calvin's judgment about the injury. "Did you come by the north bridge?"

Calvin shook his head. "My horse crossed the river. But with you ladies. . ."

"I can ride." Beatrice wanted to get to Papa's side as soon as possible.

Mama dithered in place, uncertain what to do. For a woman whose greatest concern usually involved the decision of when to change from winter wear to summer wear, she had never encountered such a challenge. "But Mama shouldn't ride."

"Perhaps we can tell Parson Cabot?" Calvin suggested.

"Excellent idea. He'll want to come, I'm sure."

"Mrs. Bailey, why don't you sit down?" Calvin led Mama to a chair as gently as if she were his own mother. "We'll take care of what needs to be done." He followed Beatrice into the front hall. "Perhaps I shouldn't have spoken so bluntly."

"You were good to come at all." Beatrice longed to put her hand to his rough cheek but refrained. "I'll gather a few things here while you go talk to the preacher. If Mama hasn't stirred, perhaps Mrs. Cabot can sit with her while we go and see Papa, you and I."

Cook bustled out of the kitchen as Calvin went out the door. "Mr. Bailey is late today. Do you want me to go ahead and serve lunch?"

At the everyday question, Mama began crying. Beatrice remained dry-eyed while she explained the situation. "Mr. Tuttle has gone to ask Mrs. Cabot to sit with my mother while I go to see Papa. We don't want to eat."

"I'll fix some tea." Cook headed back to the kitchen, but Beatrice stopped her.

"What can I bring that might help Papa?" Cook might know some folk remedies for treating injuries.

Cook clucked. "It sounds like Mr. Tuttle's got everything in hand. But if Mr. Bailey's leg is broke bad, he'll want the doctor to see to it. Otherwise, he won't walk right again. Don't you worry yourself with that. I'll get word to his clerk over at the bank, and he'll find someone to go for the doctor."

"Thank you. I'd appreciate that."

What must Papa be feeling now? Why had he sought Calvin out that morning? She wanted some answers on their way to the farm.

Beatrice explained Cook's plan when Calvin returned with the Cabots, and he nodded in acceptance. "We'd best leave the leg alone until the doctor can get here."

Mrs. Cabot fluttered around Mama. "You folks go on ahead. Stay overnight if you need to. Mrs. Bailey and I will be fine." She tucked a shawl around Mama's shoulders as if she were an invalid in need of care. With Papa injured and Mama distraught, Beatrice felt as though she had traveled from child to parent in the space of a day.

"I'll be praying for both of you as we ride," the parson promised.

Calvin took the lead on the road that led northwest out of town. "Are you going by way of the north bridge?" Beatrice asked sharply.

" 'Tis safest," Calvin said.

She turned her mare's head in the direction of the farm. "You said you found a spot to ford the river. I want to go by that route."

Calvin whipped his horse around. "I'll never forgive myself if harm comes to you while you are under my care."

"And I want to get to Papa's side as quickly as possible. Nothing will happen to me at the river." She urged her horse forward, not wanting to waste time in argument. The other horses fell in behind. A moment later, Parson Cabot came alongside. "Miss Bailey, if I may make a suggestion."

"I'm not turning back."

"No, I'm not asking you to." He spoke in the mildest of voices. "But if I do not wish to chance the river when we see how deep it is running, will you allow Calvin to lead us by another way?"

Beatrice glanced at the parson. He visited his parishioners

in all kinds of weather, fair and foul, be it day or night. She could trust him to not turn back for anything less than a truly dangerous passage. Reluctantly, she nodded.

At this point, the road widened enough for a wagon to pass into town—wide enough for the three of them to ride abreast. Beatrice wanted to ask Calvin what had prompted Papa's visit, but she hesitated to ask in front of the parson.

Parson Cabot rode with eyes that focused inward. Beatrice assumed he was praying until he said, "I can't help but wonder if God may use this difficult circumstance to resolve the dilemma the two of you have faced concerning Mr. Bailey's opposition. I have been praying for the Lord's healing, both of Mr. Bailey's body—and of the rift between you."

Calvin shook his head. "That would take a miracle. We had another argument this morning." He glanced at Beatrice, his face pale, solemn. "I fear his anger drove him to the reckless ride over the bridge."

"Did he. . .tell you not to write?" She had to ask.

"No." Calvin looked ahead to where the road wound around a corner on its way to the river. He nodded. "That's where we leave the road to get to the ford."

"So what did you argue about?" Beatrice refused to be sidetracked.

"He offered to buy my surplus seed corn for six times what I charged anyone else. I told him I would sell it to him for the same price I gave everyone else. He said I had no common sense." A wry smile twisted his mouth. "After that, I dared not speak to him of our situation. He was angered when he left, and then. . .I heard him scream." The smile disappeared, replaced by bitterness. "As if the Almighty was judging me for not accepting his help."

Or judging Papa?

"Perhaps the Almighty wanted to give both of you a second chance, without dollar signs and ears of corn coming between you," Parson Cabot said, pulling up his horse. "Isn't this where you said we leave the road?"

Once they were traveling through the trees, single file, conversation became impossible. *"That Calvin Tuttle."* Beatrice remembered how strange his name had sounded coming from Papa's lips. She couldn't help but overhear the conversation between her parents after the dinner with Mr. Perkins, since they had left the study door open.

"He knew I wanted to buy. . .going behind my back. . ." Mama's measured tones placated Papa, until Beatrice could no longer understand the words. He must have decided to go to Calvin one more time. The pair of them were too stubborn and proud for their own good. In that way the two men she loved were more alike than different. A branch smacked her in the face, and she batted another out of the way. She wouldn't tell Calvin, though. He would reject the very idea that he shared anything in common with her father.

They came upon the river suddenly. It looked quiet enough, but she had promised, so she waited for the parson to check it out.

"I believe it is safe enough to allow passage. However, Miss Bailey, your skirts. . . Mr. Tuttle, why don't you go ahead first? I will escort Miss Bailey safely across."

Calvin flushed, perhaps embarrassed by the thought of catching a glimpse of her lower limbs, but he agreed and crossed the river ahead of them. Once the trees hid him from view, Beatrice draped her skirts across her lap and the saddle horn. Her unmentionables must show beneath her petticoats, but God and people would forgive her. Her mare followed Parson Cabot into the water. The water eddied around the mare's legs as she plodded through to the other side with nary a tremor of alarm. Beatrice rearranged her skirts and smiled at the preacher.

He returned her smile. "We're ready, Mr. Tuttle."

Calvin reappeared, making sure he kept his gaze away from Beatrice's skirts. "It's this way."

They rode through fields, so empty-looking without the tree stumps. As soon as they came in sight of the cabin, Tobias crossed the field toward them.

"How fares my father?" Beatrice asked.

"Awake. Demanding to be taken home." Tobias scowled. "I'm glad you're here, Parson Cabot. Perhaps you can reason with him."

Beatrice surprised herself by laughing. "Then he must be doing fair." She caught Calvin grinning at her, and she knew that things would turn out as they should.

&

"I don't want to use the privy. Haven't you ever heard of a slop jar?"

Calvin gritted his teeth. He almost wished he had agreed to Hiram Bailey's demands and taken him home as soon as he regained strength from his accident.

"The doctor said you must exercise your leg for it to grow strong. That you need to walk." He quoted the doctor the Baileys had insisted on calling and hoped the recalcitrant patient would listen.

"I can walk around the cabin."

Calvin looked at Tobias, who shrugged. His look said, "What are you going to do about it?"

Calvin came to a decision. Plunking his hat on his head, he grabbed his hoe. "Mr. Bailey, I have offered to assist you to the privy, but you have refused my offer. We'll leave you to attend to your own needs. Tobias and I will be working in the fields until noon. We'll see you then. Good day." He slipped out the door.

Tobias followed. "Ah, sunshine and brown earth. A glorious day beckons." He eyed Calvin. "I expect any day away from the sickroom would feel glorious."

Calvin grunted. "I remind myself of what the Bible says about heaping coals of fire on his head. To do and do and do again."

"Even when he doesn't like it. I know." Tobias clapped Calvin on the shoulder. "Come, a morning's work outside will do us both good."

Calvin had to plant. If he didn't, he'd have no crop this year. They stopped by the barn, and he gestured to the barrels waiting by the feeding troughs. "Here's the final coal I'll heap on his head. I'll *give* him the extra corn. There's not much, five bushels, maybe. And he can sell it for whatever price he likes." He wanted the produce that had caused so much division and misery out of his life.

"Does your partner get a say?" Tobias teased, heaving a bag of bean seed over his shoulder. They had prepared rows for planting yesterday.

"Would you naysay me, brother?" Calvin rolled a barrel with their own corn seed toward the door.

"No, I think you're wise. Put this Year of No Summer behind us and move forward." He winked. "As long as we can do it in the company of certain ladies of our acquaintance."

Calvin bit his lip. His future with Beatrice was still far from certain, in spite of the parson's assurances that Calvin's "brave, valiant efforts to save Mr. Bailey's life"—the parson's words, not his—would not go unnoticed or unrewarded.

"We have another crop to harvest before you wed my cousin." The barrel reached the open doorway, and Calvin upended it into a wheelbarrow.

They planted their crops the way his father and grandfather had before him, corn and beans and squash growing together. The Indians had shown the first settlers the method, and so far no one had come up with a better system. Calvin had considered planting a grain like rye this year, but after the bridge's collapse, any extra money he had to invest would go into building another bridge. He had drawn up plans for a covered bridge, a toll bridge that would pay for the materials used in its construction within a year, two years at most. His arms swung in a steady rhythm while his mind raced with possibilities. Would his idea work?

"I'm going into town the day after tomorrow," Calvin told Tobias. "I have business to conduct."

At last he saw his way clear.

fourteen

Calvin whistled as he returned from town. The piece of paper crinkling in his pocket pleased his ears as much as bells on Christmas Day. The time neared when Mr. Bailey would leave the Tuttle farm, but before then, Calvin would have a serious discussion with Bea's father.

The sight of the finicky banker hobbling to the outhouse on crutches made Calvin want to chuckle, but he refrained. Instead, he held back his horse so that the man could return to the cabin in peace, unaware of an audience. Allow the man his pride. Today he would bow if need be to the one man who stood between him and Bea.

"Did you get it taken care of?" Tobias asked when he saw Calvin come out of the woods.

In answer, Calvin pulled the paper out of his vest and waved it around. "I've got it right here."

By the time they entered the cabin, Bailey had settled into a chair. He scowled at Calvin. "You chose a fine day to disappear. I told you I hoped to make it back home today."

"Yes, sir, you did. I've spoken with my uncle about that and arranged for a wagon to take you home this evening."

"About time." Bailey shifted in the chair with the grunting and mumbling that seemed a part of his every movement since the accident. He looked at Calvin, his face set in determined lines. "Not that I don't appreciate everything you've done for me. I am beholden to you." The words came out with obvious effort, against the grain of a man used to having others indebted to him and not the other way around.

Calvin took a seat opposite him and spread open the paper he had brought back from the bank. "I wished to speak with you, sir, regarding a matter of concern to us both."

"I suppose you mean my daughter. Beatrice Alice."

Calvin didn't answer directly. "Before I spoke with you, I wanted to come to you as a free man. That's why I was gone this morning. I went to the bank and paid off the lien on the property. You are not beholden to me, sir, but neither am I beholden to you. Not now."

Bailey studied the paper. "I suppose you had cash from the sale of your corn."

"And other things." He cleared his throat. "I know you are concerned that a farmer such as myself cannot provide for your daughter. So I've spent a good bit of time over the past weeks considering my financial situation." He sent up a short prayer. Would this idea work, his effort to reach out to Mr. Bailey in the language he understood best?

"This amount"—Calvin opened his book of accounts and pointed to the head of the first column of figures—"shows how much cash I have on hand after settling the debt with the bank." The second column read EXPENSES. "This is how much I expect to spend this year."

Bailey frowned. "That seems a trifle high."

"Not after I buy what I need to construct a covered bridge. I wanted to last year, and I'm sorry I didn't. I regret your accident and refuse to let it happen again to someone else."

Bailey harrumphed.

"But see here." The third column read INCOME. "By the fall, I will receive income from a small toll for crossing the bridge, as well as profit from this year's crop. If all goes as expected, my investment could double within twelve months."

Bailey leaned back, his face a mask, the one Calvin had seen when he had gone to him pleading for money to start up his farm. "This house is hardly more than a shack."

"But it won't always be that way. I'm sure you've heard the story about how my mother's family lived in a cave for part of the war, and now see their home. If your daughter marries me, sir, she may not always live in luxury—but she will never be in need. So help me God."

"And the extra seed corn you have on hand?" Bailey asked.

Would the man never let go of that corn? "I will give it to you, and you can do whatever you wish with it."

A small smile played around Bailey's lips. "I will pay you $1.50 a bushel. And I won't accept a penny less."

A dollar and a half? Could Calvin live with that? The seed wasn't worth that much, but. . . "I'll accept your terms."

"Very well." Bailey extended his hand. "You have treated me better than I deserve, Mr. Tuttle. And you appear to be a man of good business sense, as well as a man with the welfare of the community in his heart. If you choose to call on my daughter again, I will not stand in your way."

❧

The community of Maple Notch gathered to help Calvin with the bridge raising, and Beatrice couldn't wait to join the festivities. She put on his favorite pink dress. She had stitched a special sampler to present him on this auspicious occasion. SEEDTIME AND HARVEST HAVE NOT CEASED; A BRIDGE TO LOVE PROVIDES THE FEAST. The barn-like structure she had fashioned spanned a rippling brook, with lilac bushes growing on the banks, and was titled TUTTLE BRIDGE, 1817.

"Are you ready?" Papa came to the foot of the stairs. A slight limp was the only reminder of the awful accident that could have cost his life. Something had happened during his recovery; she couldn't believe the change in him.

"I've never seen you go to a barn raising before," she teased. Dressed as he was in Wellington boots and plain breeches, he didn't look like himself. She couldn't remember the last time she had seen him dressed in anything other than a waistcoat and trousers.

"We've never had a bridge raising in Maple Notch before. You look lovely, my dear." He offered her his arm. "I trust my appearance doesn't distress you."

"Not at all." She kissed his cheek. "I am proud of you."

The sun dappled the leaves of the trees, so very *green*, so right for the state of the *Verts Monts*—"Green Mountains." Beatrice inhaled the scent of bursting growth and fresh air, the feel of sunshine warming her skin, the sight of green deepening from the palest, almost white stems to the full-blown green of new grass. The Year of No Summer had passed, and 1817 promised to be a season of unparalleled growth.

But nothing mattered more to her than the man waiting at the bridge. As soon as they rounded the corner where they could see the river, Calvin stood out from all the others with his broad shoulders and his voice raised in instructions on the bridge building.

An invisible thread pulled his head in their direction as they approached. A smile as wide as the open sky bloomed on his face, and he ran toward the wagon. "Bea, Mr. Bailey. I've been waiting for you." He put his strong hands around Beatrice's waist and lifted her from the wagon. "With your permission, sir, there's something I want to show your daughter."

Papa nodded, and Calvin tugged her toward the stack of lumber waiting for the bridge raising. "There is something I must show you." He took her to the back of the pile, to a single log stretched between two tree stumps. What could he find so exciting about a piece of wood?

"You know the story of how my mother's family hid out in a cave during the Revolutionary War, and how Grandfather Tuttle was a Tory who didn't want his only surviving son to marry a patriot."

Beatrice nodded her head. Children from Maple Notch still camped out in the Reids' cave. But what did that have to do with the plank stretched out before them?

"And you probably know Pa helped them with their farm that summer."

Again Beatrice nodded.

"Pa told me about this once, but I had never seen it until I started cutting the timber we needed for the bridge. Look."

He pointed to the faded and scarred spot on the fresh-planed wood. Someone had carved something into the living wood years ago. Squinting, she managed to make out the letters. JT and SR. "Josiah Tuttle and Sally Reid."

"My parents. Their love crossed a chasm of divided loyalties and war and created a legacy that they passed on to me. I'm going to put this where everyone can see." He went down on one knee and took her hand in his. "Can we do the same, Miss Beatrice Alice Bailey? Can we build a bridge of love that will overcome the difficulties, whether natural or manmade, that come our way, with the help of the Lord?" He reached into his pocket and set a pocketknife on his palm.

Giddiness swept through her. She stilled her thoughts, her heart, her hands, and took the knife in her right hand. Bending over the board, she drove a straight line and added two loops. . .B. Again. B. A simple plus sign.

As her hand began the hard lines of the curve, she felt Calvin's hand settle over hers. He stood beside her, guiding her fingers as they carved a C and a T.

He studied her, his eyes dark with passion, and she felt breathless.

"My answer is. . ."

He took her hands in his.

"Yes."

A Letter To Our Readers

Dear Reader:
In order that we might better contribute to your reading
enjoyment, we would appreciate your taking a few minutes
to respond to the following questions. We welcome your
comments and read each form and letter we receive. When
completed, please return to the following:

Fiction Editor
Heartsong Presents
PO Box 719
Uhrichsville, Ohio 44683

1. Did you enjoy reading *Bridge to Love* by Darlene Franklin?
   ❏ Very much! I would like to see more books by this author!
   ❏ Moderately. I would have enjoyed it more if

   _____

   _____

   _____

2. Are you a member of **Heartsong Presents**? ❏ Yes ❏ No
   If no, where did you purchase this book? _____

   _____

3. How would you rate, on a scale from 1 (poor) to 5 (superior),
   the cover design? _____

4. On a scale from 1 (poor) to 10 (superior), please rate the
   following elements.

   ____ Heroine   ____ Plot
   ____ Hero   ____ Inspirational theme
   ____ Setting   ____ Secondary characters

5. These characters were special because? _____

_____

_____

6. How has this book inspired your life? _____

_____

_____

7. What settings would you like to see covered in future
   Heartsong Presents books? _____

_____

_____

8. What are some inspirational themes you would like to see
   treated in future books? _____

_____

_____

9. Would you be interested in reading other **Heartsong
   Presents** titles? ❑ Yes   ❑ No

10. Please check your age range:
    ❑ Under 18   ❑ 18-24
    ❑ 25-34   ❑ 35-45
    ❑ 46-55   ❑ Over 55

Name _____

Occupation _____

Address _____

City, State, Zip _____

E-mail _____

THE BLACKSMITH'S BRAVERY

A reformed saloon girl and decent markswoman, Vashti Edwards earns the opportunity to drive stagecoach, but blacksmith Griffin Bane fears for her safety—and his growing attraction—as the line becomes repeatedly targeted by robbers. Can The Ladies' Shooting Club catch the bandits and bring the stubborn couple together?

Historical, paperback, 320 pages, 5.1875" x 8"

Heartsong

HEARTSONG PRESENTS TITLES AVAILABLE NOW:

Presents

Great Inspirational Romance at a Great Price!

Heartsong Presents books are inspirational romances in contemporary and historical settings, designed to give you an enjoyable, spirit-lifting reading experience. You can choose wonderfully written titles from some of today's best authors like Wanda E. Brunstetter, Mary Connealy, Susan Page Davis, Cathy Marie Hake, Joyce Livingston, and many others.

When ordering quantities less than six, above titles are $3.99 each.
Not all titles may be available at time of order.

HEARTSONG PRESENTS

DISCARD

If you love Christian romance…

$12.99

inspi... Heartsong Presents'

toda... ...da E. Brunstetter,
Mar... ...Marie Hake, and
Joyce Livingston, to mention a...

When you join Heartsong Presents, you'll enjoy four brand-new, mass-market, 176-page books—two contemporary and two historical—that will build you up in your faith when you discover God's role in every relationship you read about!

Mass Market 176 Pages

Imagine…four new romances every four weeks—with men and women like you who long to meet the one God has chosen as the love of their lives…all for the low price of $12.99 postpaid.

To join, simply visit www.heartsong presents.com or complete the coupon below and mail it to the address provided.

✄- -

YES! Sign me up for Heartsong!

NEW MEMBERSHIPS WILL BE SHIPPED IMMEDIATELY!
Send no money now. We'll bill you only $12.99 postpaid with your first shipment of four books. Or for faster action, call 1-740-922-7280.

NAME_____

ADDRESS_____

CITY_____ STATE _____ ZIP _____

MAIL TO: HEARTSONG PRESENTS, P.O. Box 721, Uhrichsville, Ohio 44683
or sign up at **WWW.HEARTSONGPRESENTS.COM**